T0171515

Order this book online at www.trafford.com
or email orders@trafford.com

Most Trafford titles are also available at major online book retailers.

Note for Librarians: A cataloguing record for this book is available from Library and Archives Canada at www.collectionscanada.ca/amicus/index-e.html

Printed in Victoria, BC, Canada.

ISBN: 978-1-4269-1397-6 (sc)
ISBN: 978-1-4269-1396-9 (hc)

Library of Congress Control Number: 2009936241

Our mission is to efficiently provide the world's finest, most comprehensive book publishing service, enabling every author to experience success. To find out how to publish your book, your way, and have it available worldwide, visit us online at www.trafford.com

Trafford rev. 09/02/09

www.trafford.com

North America & international
toll-free: 1 888 232 4444 (USA & Canada)
phone: 250 383 6864 ♦ fax: 812 355 4082

Dedication:

This story would not have been possible without the combination of energy from many people: the art of Aisleen Romano, the editing of Kimberley Arnold, and the support of many friends. Without your help making this into the work of art it is, it would be just another book.

Chapter One:

Once upon a time:

Cain:

It was a beautiful spring day; the air warm and the road very rough from the spring run-off. Maybe it was the warmth after the long winter that set his eyes to roaming the green fields, or maybe the sky or the beautiful mountains. It doesn't matter what it was that distracted him or why he was distracted; it only matters that he was distracted. It was this distraction, more than anything else, that changes his life as a quiet mountain woodsman because, when he looks back to the road, there is a child standing there, staring at the oncoming horses, his hand in his mouth, the horses bearing down, only a few meters to stop or turn the wagon before running him down.

He reacts instantly, his hands on the reins, casting about collecting the horses, pulling them to the left ditch to avoid the youngster. The load of logs hits the shoulder and starts to slide into the ditch. He pulls the horses the other way, trying to stop his load from overturning. Once past the stunned boy he pulls the heavy load back onto the road, his wagon bouncing in and over the ditches on the right of the road as he overcompensates and is just able to pull them all to a stop before the jostling load overturns.

With a relieved whoosh of breath Cain wipes his dripping wet brow and, once the shaking stops, he climbs down off the wagon.

He stomps in anger, intent upon scolding the boy about playing in the road. He raises his hand to point at the child, litany on the tip of his tongue, when a young woman is there, between him and his target.

Facing him, hands on her hips, dangerous passion on her face. "What do you think you're doing? Racing so fast down the road, don't you look where you are going? My brother was standing there a long time before you came, and you almost kill him with your horses and all this wood. Why are you in such a hurry anyways? Where is the fire?"

Taken completely by surprise by her sudden appearance, he hears himself babbling, "I was …then he was…then you…" He cannot make himself meet her eyes so filled with indignant fire, this raging woman.

He notices other things too: her shining fine black hair, and her slim feminine body.

Ana:

She does not pause in her tirade. "Are you crazy? Driving like a crazy person not watching the road. I bet your mind was miles away! You driving this thing so fast and careless, you could have killed us…"

It is then, as she pauses for breath, that she notices his strong shoulders hunched as if under an attack, his open and pacifying hands up to staunch the verbal assault. With her mouth open to continue she is stopped by his upturned face.

Their eyes meet, and in that moment of suspended time they both know in their hearts from that moment on they are fated to be forever together. Three things happen all at once then: her anger is gone, his fear is gone, and there is a small spark of electricity that travels between their hearts.

"What is your name?" he asks.

"Ana," she answers.

"I am Cain," he tells her.

Two years pass.

Cain and Ana are betrothed. The wedding is set for the first festival in the spring when fate changes everything.

Cain:

One dark night, a terrible night, with a cold wind rattling the windows and stealing the warmth from the fire, comes a knock on the door of his small cottage.

'Who could be out on a night like this?' Cain thinks as he rises from his chair stepping to the door. The cold is intense, the wind a blast around the frame, chilling his face and hands, reaching beneath his warm shirt to touch his heart with chill fingers.

Sliding the bar back to open the room to the elements a dread touches him. He hesitates for an instant, and in that moment he teeters on the edge of chance. The door hinges pivot not just the door but destiny.

As the door swings open his fate becomes sealed.

He swings the door wide and looks out into the night. At first he sees nothing. As the deeper darkness reaches into the house from the doorway, a feminine formed shadow oozes into the room to take the floor; sliding effortlessly, a mix of substance and ethereal presence. Her black garment drifts and flutters, seeming to fill the whole room, but she stays near the door.

Startled and upset now Cain backs away from the apparition, backing into the chair before the fire, a room once cozy and warm seconds ago, now without any warmth.

The apparition hovers forward into the room, her arm extended.

Ana:

As she works at her chores she daydreams. She knows it is only a matter of time until she may be with Cain. Expertly folding the laundry the clothes all but fly to her will, then off to the innumerable other chores that make up the time for her. With her mind mostly free, she can think and dream of her future and his.

Evening arrives with a pleasant dinner and warm chatter in her home.

After dinner a feeling comes over her, at first an itch; had she forgotten to do something? Then the itch becomes more of a feeling of foreordination. Something is going to happen.

The weather had gotten worse as the day edged toward evening, and from the draft through the house she knew it was going to be a bad night. She could not settle.

In her restlessness she opens the front door after putting on her shawl. She was shocked and then her dread deepened to see the thick black clouds flowing from the sky to cover the mountains like thick black honey. She fears now not for the cold or weather but for her Cain and his mother alone on the mountain.

With a tremulous hand she closes the door.

Ana is strong; once the shock has left her she knows what she must do.

Bustling through the house now, she gathers the things she will need; she calls for her brother as she walks to her father's chair in the den. "Father, Cain needs me. I can feel it."

Ana's father, a tailor by trade, knows from many a time with Ana's mother that when the women of his house feel things they are most often right, thus to restrain the women over something as simple as common sense or reason is pure folly on his part; he would only slow the operation and end up with a houseful of worried women. "Ana, go with my blessing but take your brother, and Stony, he will see you safe in this foul weather. Hurry home my little one."

She bends down and kisses him on the nose.

Collecting her brother and the stout little pony, she heads out for the mountain road and whatever fate has placed in her way.

Once out in the storm she pushes the small pony to a jog.

Her brother keeps up easily with his long stride and light step, his bow strung and ready in his hand, his long hunter's knife at his side. She catches his eye; he is grinning and there is the flash of adventure upon him. She shivers. There are things that make you cold and then there are things that make you quake inside: her brother's smile made her shiver. There has always been a bit too much of the feral in her brother... a bit of the woods left behind his eyes. As always he does not speak. He has a tongue and when he does speak his voice is often rough from disuse. But there is no need between them; she knows what he is thinking.

There is evil in this night.

All the while the clouds settle lower, making the mountain disappear in a black swirling mass.

Cain:

The witch is quite close to him now. Without seeming to move she is there, her hand stroking the air near his face.

"I know what you want -- your heart is clear to me. Your place in life makes you unhappy. Your destiny you would change if you could." Her hand is now a perfect yet accusing finger.

He sees now beneath the swirling midnight robes a coldly beautiful visage, her white teeth flashing with reflected light as her words slam into him. He backs away further, pushing his chair back to the wall. The crash of the chair into the hearth wall ends his flight.

With dread he recognizes this witch although he has never seen her. Only word of her has ever reached his ears on his trips to market: stories of a black form offering false cures or bringing plague. His mind races. How does this woman, a stranger to him, know his deepest inner doubts and wishes? He has told no one and has kept it buried deep.

"I can help you, Cain Woodsman. I can give you all that you desire and much more..."

Her perfect hand rotates over and in its palm there is a huge white pearl. Bigger than his fist yet perfectly held in her open palm, as though glued there.

More than that it seems to give off a light, and as his eyes are drawn to it, the light changes to images, the images moving and organizing. He sees himself in an ermine robe, a beautiful blond princess at his side.

Ana:

A short distance up the mountain road the wind builds, blowing in their faces, making every inch of progress hard won. Then the snow starts. Too late in the season for snow, and with the wind and biting cold, Ana knows there is more happening here than a simple storm.

Powers are working to keep her away from Cain this night.

Doubts begin to assail her. What if she is just worried for nothing? What if the clouds are just clouds? It would not be the first time she had seen them descend like this; why does she fear now?

Why is she here on this cold night, on a pony racing up the mountain, to save a man like her Cain? A man, she is sure, who can take care of himself and his mother very well indeed as he has done for many years; why now, she asks herself.

Her brother starts to slow, his tread uncertain and his head down, shoulders hunched. With a far distance to go she considers sending him home if for no other reason than his seeming pleasure in the darkness of the night. It again gives her that coldness in her heart, like there is more to her brother's accompanying her than she knows.

She could go on alone but something holds her back; some shadow or feeling won't let her place herself alone on this road. Though a good pony, Stony would not help if she ran into wolves but her brother's stout bow and sure eye would. Hunching down over Stony's neck as much for warmth as for assurance, she clucks softly to the little pony and they pick up speed again, even against the ever present wind.

At the next to last turn to Cain's cabin her fear is realized: out of the wind rises a howl, then another, closing in on them. The pony shies and snorts as the next howl seems to come from just ahead.

Cain:

Even in the cold air from the open door, Cain sweats profusely; droplets glisten on his brow and fall into his eyes. He can feel the emanations of power from this woman. As he looks at the orb, feelings and images flood his mind: he sees himself in the finest clothes on a prancing horse with gold and silver on his saddle.

But in the images are shadows of the cost for this: the men surrounding him for protection; the people in the image are all sad or angry; even his men look with greed upon what he has.

"This can be yours: wealth, power, land and a beautiful wife." In her other hand is now a small cherry, ripe and sweet looking. She holds it by its stem, dangling it between her fingers. She steps further into the room, the fruit dangling closer and closer. Cain, unable to look away, is captivated by the pearl and this beautiful woman. Doubts slip away in the flow of her words and the soft susurrations of her magic.

"Just open your lips, accept this gift, and it will all be yours." She is close now. He can see her face, its cold beauty and lust, her black lips, brown eyes, and flashing feral teeth. She is before him now, the cherry almost at his lips.

Ana:

They started as shapes around the trees, the small candle lantern she carries turning them into stalking shadows, one here, one there. Her brother, arrow nocked, being careful to make his small store last, waits for more than shadows. Stony, edgy and nervous, is quite aware of what wolves are, but remains brave beneath Ana.

On the last turn, the light of the open door becomes visible; she pushes Stony faster. There is a sudden motion from the right side of the road, the shape there reminding Ana of a nightmare she had had as a girl: blackness deeper than the shadows around it, surreal in its size, its form brings despair as a cloud. Bright white teeth in slavering jaws, its red eyes track her as it moves to block her path.

With a gleam in its eye and a sound deep in its chest, the wolf lowers its head and sniffs for a space of time easier measured in thought than in any true span of time, for it may not have been any time at all. Later Ana put the events into a blur and buried them deep for the fodder of terror-ridden dreams.

The wolf turns from her and locks eyes with her brother. For an instant, there is a resemblance between her beloved brother and this thing from hell, a kinship that should not be.

Her brother pulls back and shoots just as the giant beast launches to the attack. The arrow plunges into the gaping maw.

The wolf falls to the road dead. The other wolves, seeing their leader struck down, slink back into the trees to await another opportunity to feast.

Ana pushes off the little pony and races for the open door to the cabin flooding light into the night. No doubts left in her mind, she enters the cabin.

What awaits her there is a shock: Cain backed up against his favorite chair, the chair pushed from its normal place in front of the hearth, his eyes wide and mouth open, a bright cherry above his mouth, and the woman in black.

The woman turns her head and with her eyes, freezes Ana to the spot. Ana's eyes plead with Cain, not to do what he is about to do.

The woman in black sneers and mashes the cherry into Cain's open mouth.

They both disappear.

From the back room an old woman emerges, and with bewilderment calls out, "Cain, are you out here?"

Chapter Two

Ana:

*A*na takes Cain's mother, loading a few of the old woman's possessions on the pony, and with her brother guarding their backs, she leaves the mountain returning to her family's home in the valley.

She feels as she leaves the small home that she will never return.

Ana's father is waiting in the yard as the bedraggled trio arrives. From one look into her father's eyes she sees relief mingled with apprehension and a lot of questions. "Hello, Papa," she says as she hugs him. "Let's go inside. We have a lot to tell you."

That afternoon, her father speaks to the other men of the village, telling them what had happened to his children the previous night. A group of men are sent up the mountain to see for themselves in the light of day what has befallen the woodsman. They find the great wolf and bring it to the village. They also find the vacant cottage and no sign of Cain.

Upon their arrival back from the mountain, Ana's brother is acclaimed as the great wolf killer and much praise is laid upon him that killed such a great beast. This is also when he is given the name Lupul Ucigas which is a great and noble name, a name that bears with it the mixed honor of its kind: Wolf Slayer.

Even after everyone hears the story there is still debate as to what actually happened to Cain. Was he carried off by a witch as Ana and her brother believe? Or did he abandon them all? Some of the old men of the village still remember Cain's father and the strangeness of his disappearance when Cain was a baby. Maybe

Ana is telling this tale to hide her despair that he would leave her, perhaps for another woman?

The village is awash with the gossip. By evening most of the village, women and men alike, have convinced themselves the latter is much more likely than the former; what would a witch want with a woodsman? A lot of doubt still surfaces; Ana is much loved in the village and very few people would dare to doubt her word.

The next day the sun rises as it always has, the cows and sheep beg for their feed, people perform the tasks of daily living as they always have, but today there is a difference. Today it is decided that an envoy be sent to the castle in hopes that the good king may be able to help find the lost woodsman.

Ana is angry, a simmering anger rooted in suspicions. He was taken from her by witchcraft! The moment plays over and over in her mind: his eyes reaching for her, her arm outstretched, but she could not reach him in time to save him. Her heart had been ripped from her chest when he had vanished in a flicker of light before her eyes, taken from her. His eyes, the small turn to his mouth when he smiles, his little secret smile, taken from her. Yes, anger!

With that anger in her eyes she stands before the village. "I must know what has become of him. I will go!"

None dare dispute her right to go, Cain and she being all but married.

Ana's brother decides to go as well. At 15 the way the girls look at him makes him uneasy now especially with his new celebrity. He thinks it's ok for certain girls to show interest in him now, but every available woman in the village looks at him differently now. Where he was but a child two days ago now the village considers him a man. He has proven his skills and this makes him attractive to not just the young girls his age but to the older women as well. He gladly accepts the chance to go away for a while.

Cain's mother: living for the last few years in a quiet fog of early senility, her mind drifting loose from the shore of reality by the loss of her husband, her only tether to reality is Cain. Her life had been the slow easy workings of a solitary farm, the care of her son, the small stock they needed, and her knitting... until later when Cain cared for her. This is her world, so she is very disturbed and shaken by the events of the past day. Rising from her sleep she is more engaged in her life than she has been for years. She knows with a keen mind that her son is gone. She doesn't know why or where but she misses him. She is not well known in the village but her knitting is legendary. The tightness and warmth of her work makes the few pieces she has sold over the years the owner's family prized possessions. For this and the fact that she had lived alone with her son makes her a bit of an oddity for the village.

She cannot be dissuaded from going along!

No one else will go with them. As Ana turns to face those around her none will meet her eye. Cain was not well known.

Ana's father gives her the pony, the brave little Stony that had stood and faced the great wolf. She hugs her father and tells him she will send him home along with her brother as soon as she reaches the castle. With a look she tells him she will not be coming home unless Cain is by her side. He hugs her tight, his tears dampening her collar.

It is the fourth morning after Cain's abduction. Packed for travel, the pony loaded, two women dressed for the cool days and frigid nights and a young man with bow upon his back give their last farewells to the few friends that are there.

With a look to the road, they begin the long march on the market road to the castle, many days and nights away.

The road is a dirt and cobble path through the valleys, winding around large rocks and even larger trees, following brooks and wending up hills too steep to climb straight. All day they walk on.

Occasionally Ana will speak to the old woman; she answers the questions but there is a gloom to the procession that conversation cannot dispel, so the answers are short and do not lend to continuance.

As the sun sets on their first day of travel, Lupul picks a spot under a large beech tree as their first campsite. They break bread and share the fire Ana makes from some fallen branches and her tinder box. Around the fire they sit; the old woman takes out her knitting and Lupul rubs oil into the wood of his bow. Ana spends the time looking off into the night thinking of other times, missing Cain. Soon they bank the fire and set their blankets, preparing for sleep. Lupul sits a silent watch across from the women.

A small sprite from the forest comes to her ear, sitting beside her it sings quietly to her to wake her and get her attention without distracting Lupul from his duty on the other side of the fire with his bow and sharp arrows. Ana awakes slowly and is not completely sure she is awake as the beautiful singing brings her back from her dreams. The sprite changes its singing as it sees Ana's eyes open.

"Heart of gold to heart of stone
Beware the heart, save hearts from home
In the mountain dies a warm heart
In the castle lies a cold hearth."

With the last strains, the fairy takes wing and is gone in a flicker of the eye.

The next day she can't seem to remember where she heard the little jingle she can't seem to get out of her head.

The day drags longer as they become aware of the aches and pains of the previous day's travel.

Today sees them in a continuous uphill trek over the mountain ridges, the climb adding strain to joints and feet still getting acclimated for the march. So, it is with the sun still lingering in the evening, they all but drop from exhaustion as they reach the first flat place for hours and decide to make camp.

Ana makes the fire again, this time under an ancient oak. The fire is warm and welcoming as she takes out their dinner and heats it by the fire: sausages with cheese, bread and honey. After eating Ana heats some water and makes a tea of comfrey and peppermint. The old woman sits with her eyes distant, sipping the tea, then as in old habit she takes out the needles and begins her knitting. Ana again wanders off with her mind as Lupul takes out the bow to once again carefully oil its limbs.

This night there is a visitor to their camp.

An old cloaked man walks from the wood and settles across the fire from Ana. So silent and quick his motion, it is a few moments before Ana comes back to herself and notices. "This task is not for you." He states as Ana looks up, startled.

Gasping and clutching for his hunting knife Lupul tenses for the spring.

The old man raises a hand, open and placating he gestures for him to settle back down. The old man's face is wrapped in the cowl of his heavy dark robes; he reaches up and pushes the hood back. Later Ana can only remember his eyes: black within black, pools of dark liquid.

Putting his walking stick across his knees he speaks to her. "You are young and life is bright in you; forget him and take another for your love." He smiles a warm compassionate smile showing the wrinkles of many years.

A quiet cackle crosses the fire from Cain's mother, "You would have us go home and forget my son so easy?"

With this the old man turns his attention from Ana, "You do not go to your son; you go to your death. Your son is no more. Take my warning and abandon this futile quest."

To Ana, "Your heart is not all you will lose if you continue. Love, if not forsaken, will be a dagger at your throat."

He turns to Lupul, "Your path has many branches, and this is but a short stem that leads to sorrow and a dead end. You must turn from it. There are others that need you more."

From the cold night, there is heard far off the lonely call of a wolf. The old man raises a finger. "They speak your name and they tell of the debt you owe. Soon they will not just speak so. Theirs is not a life of patience."

With this last he reaches to the tea and pours himself a small portion, wraps his hands around the cup and settles back against the tree, sipping.

Indignant, Ana asks, "Who are you? Why do you tell us these things? They do not matter to us. If anything your words tell us that Cain needs us dearly. I will not step one foot from the path that leads me to him." There is fire in her eye as she spits this last at him.

Finishing his tea there is a glint of humor in his eye; it is gone as quickly as it came and Ana could not say later if it was there at all. "I must go now, my message is complete. If you persist, my brother will meet you outside the tower gates in three days. He is your last chance; listen to him if you will not to me." With this last he rises to his feet, steps to the trees and is gone in one breath.

In the morning the weather turns bad. Looking ahead over their dried meat and travel bread, the sun shows them a solid wall of rain to the north and a clear sky to the south, the way home. Ana stands, carefully puts away her blankets and wraps herself close in her warmest coat, hood up. She never again looks back or has any doubts of her path. Lupul unstrings his bow, packing the waxed gut string carefully into a pocket and covers the bow in a wrapping oil cloth. All prepared the trio take to the road and head into the downpour.

Night and day the weather stays with them, the water getting into everything, down necks and dampening socks. Each night the fire is smaller and colder and they have to go further back into the woods to find dry tinder.

Making the nights even longer they begin to see things. They are being followed. Lupul is the first to discover this as he searches the trees for a place to camp on the fourth night; it is stealthy and quick but he sees the shape, far back in the darkness and shadows followed by another glimpse later on the road. That night he takes the watch. Regardless of the rain, he strings his bow and keeps his arrows close. The next day dawns cold, the weather making the night cling and the dawn claw its way through the clouds. Ahead over the rise Ana glimpses the castle on its mountain in the north, and then it is drowned in the gloom of the day. They have another day of marching ahead but the possibility of a dry, warm welcome at the castle spurs them on through the torrent. As if knowing this, the rain becomes a solid wall of water, drowning out talk and pressing down on them like a cold, wet blanket, making them blindly grope for the road. At noon the tactics change and a wind blowing from the north turns the rain into sleet and hail, blowing horizontally into their faces.

Unable to continue into the wind, they form a line and take each other's coat tail, following the pony as Lupul leads it, head down, single file. It is almost nightfall when they reach the gates. Closed and barred, seemingly deserted, no one answers Lupul's pounding, forcing the trio to seek shelter back in the forest under a spreading old oak.

No sooner had they picked the spot when the rain and sleet stop, presenting a suddenly quiet surrounding to the great tree. For the first time in three days they build a regular fire and make soup with the last of their dried meat, some mushrooms and a small cabbage, to warm them and drive back the darkness.

When the soup is gone and they are sitting around the fire sipping the peppermint comfrey tea, a form separates from the darkness behind the tree and quickly sits on a root beside the fire across from Ana.

Warned of this visitor Lupul does not stiffen but his hand does slide to his knife, and his eyes scan for others around the gloom. This creature also takes the form of an old man and again is dark robed with a narrow face and eyes black within black. His wrinkled face tells of many years and much pain. "What fools you are. Make your beds and sleep well; tomorrow will be the last for you, good mother," he scoffs. Then, in mocking jest, "Your shoes will walk farther than you."

To Ana he turns and with intensity rasps, "Love is not honorable for you." With a half smile he adds, "Your eyes and your hands will do what your heart cannot."

Turning to Lupul, "You may not enter here! This you may not do!"

Turning back to Ana he says, "Since you have chosen this path I may only help you twice more. After tonight three moons from now you shall meet me by this tree and I will answer three questions that you will ask then, but only three!"

His eyes water and voice rises as if to cover deep emotion. "Your love is no more. When you see him the soul you seek will not look out at you. Beware him; he is no friend of yours. He will use you and there will be no regret, remorse or tenderness, only pain. Once you face this and harden your heart you will survive. Heed this warning and we shall meet again in one month. Not and you will die in a month." Like his brother he stands, turns and is gone back behind the great tree.

Dawn rides in like a knight, ripping and trampling the darkness. Into this dawn three travelers trek, their destination reached, but the journey just begun.

Ana, freshly dressed in her clean garments and special cloak and shoes, Cain's mother in her clean clothes and Lupul in his best hunting clothes with bow wrapped and stored on his back, string in pocket, his knife hidden beneath his cloak and the folds of his shirt. They approach the gate, the portcullis having risen moments before and the great doors swung asunder. The farmers and craftsmen with their carts are already streaming back to the bend in the road.

Two attempts have taught them the necessity of patience as when they approach the gate they are warned off by the haggard and threatening looks of the cart pushers, the hill being a steep climb to the main gate and all the wagons heavy. Some pushed by men or women others hauled by horse, oxen or pony. So they wait by the gate for the press of vendors to subside.

As the morning wears on and the line remains stationary, it is clear that something is wrong. Murmurs spread down the line. Lupul creeps to the side of one of the wagons and overhears discussion between one of the wagoners and a guard.

"...new tax from the new lord," the guard says.

"You mean we have to pay to enter the gate now? A tax to enter the castle?" Outrage and apprehension are clear in his voice.

"What nonsense is this? As I told you! You cannot pass without paying the entrance tax. It's a new law from the king's new advisor. It's not much, just pay it and be done, and then you can come in and go about your affairs," the guard says with rolled eyes and the look of a man talking to idiots.

Lupul slinks back to the women, "There is a new tax to enter the castle. It has everything backed up. Do we have money for this?"

Ana looks at her brother, "I don't know, how much is it?"

Lupul slinks back to his place by the wagon and listens in. In a few moments he returns. They discuss the money and decide they only have enough for two of them to enter.

Lupul looks at his sister and then the old woman. "The old man was right, I cannot go here."

"You must make your way home. Tell them that we made it and that we will be home soon." She hugs her brother close and kisses him on each cheek.

Cain's mother says, "Thank you for taking us here. Journey well, my boy." She also hugs him and kisses him on each cheek. He turns from the women and begins the long trek home.

As the road and gate finally clear and the sun reaches its height in the heaven, the two women, supporting each other, make their way to the gate of the castle.

"You must pay the tax to enter the castle," greets the guard almost lazily now as the women enter and approach the great door. He takes their money and asks their business. "What do you two want here?"

Ana steps up and tells of their plight. She asks if the guard has seen Cain.

The guard chuckles and scratches his jaw, "I do not recall seeing anyone like you describe passing this gate, but there are four gates to the castle; he might have passed at any." He waves his arm for them to go on into the castle.

What awaits them as they pass the great door is at once amazing and depressing for the women. Crowds of people are in the streets now, the noise and bustle intimidates the women. Coming from a small village they are not used to the large number of people doing business all around them. The noise of the vendors calling their wares, the chickens, hogs, dogs, and children all create a cacophony of sounds and smells. Ana almost backs out to run home to her small farm and quiet life. Then her mind runs to Cain and what he may be going through and she stiffens her back. There is only forward for her.

The crowd is boisterous but not hostile and they make their way easily through the throng, working their way up the main road of the castle into the commons, a clustering of houses lining the inside of the walls before the main castle keep.

Ana notices the houses are of a different stone than the outer walls and marvels at the colors and designs. As they round the common, there is a commotion at the second gate.

From the entrance comes a clatter of hooves; three horses sweep in bearing down on Ana and the old woman.

Ana is shocked, not from the horses, she has been around animals her whole life; it is who she sees on the second horse that shocks her. Clothed in a bright red tunic and dark brown wool hose, wrapped in a light blue cloak and wearing leather shoes cut for riding, is Cain!

In an instant she reaches for him, standing in the middle of the roadway. Almost too late, she turns to step from the path but the old woman is slower. Ana is only halfway to safety when the first horse pushes her to the wall hard.

The impact is to her head and that is all she knows as her sight goes dark.

When she regains consciousness, she is on her side leaning against the wall, her things gone, with a group of children looking down at her.

The children scatter as they see her blink and hear her moans. She slowly turns from the wall and rises to her knees then to her feet, perceptions sliding around her mind like marbles in a bucket,

Then it all comes clear in a crash and she cries out, "Cain! Oh, Cain! Why?"

In front of her is a shapeless heap of clothing. She lurches to the old woman, crying out and waving her arms to chase off the dogs sniffing the corpse. It is Cain's mother; she lies on her face in the cobbles, her legs and arms splayed out around her. She pulls the woman to the edge of the road and cradling her in her arms, she cries.

She is on the grass in the town center when next she is aware; she doesn't remember how she got there or losing consciousness, but now that she is awake it must have been so. Sitting up she sees a woman in the doorway of a small shop across the road. The woman beckons to Ana. With nowhere else to go, and her mind still unsteady, she staggers to her feet. Leaving the dead woman's body she makes her way to the doorway. The woman takes her arm and leads her inside.

Chapter Three

Ana:

Ana wakes slowly; she turns over to face the room. Beside her on a small box is a tray with bread, cheese and water. In a moment there is nothing left but crumbs.

She feels much more restored after the food and attempts to get to her feet; her legs are very weak and her head reels. She sits back and looks around her. She is in a small, dark room with bales of cloth piled to the ceiling everywhere except a path from the door to her small cot. This gives the impression the room is a lot smaller than it is. The air is stale and warm, smelling of the cloth and the bare earth. There is a rug on the floor she notices, woven of course hair. She forces herself to try getting to her feet; she must answer the questions that now clamor in her waking mind. Where is she? What has become of Cain and his mother's remains? The dear woman; to die so close to finding her son. Then the memory sharpens and the realization comes that it was Cain's horse that had pushed her to the wall and trampled his own mother. The Cain she knew would have prostrated himself in sorrow at the thought of such a thing. She remembers all he did to stop the wagon from striking her brother. She must be wrong. That could not have been Cain.

Her feet slowly return to her and with them her wonder at the cloth around her. She reaches out and feels the bolts of soft spun wools and wishes the light were better so she could see the colors.

She wanders her way through the piles and soon finds the curtain to the front of the building. She pushes it aside to a stunningly bright reception of color and activity. The shop front is open to the street now, and there are people bustling and pushing everywhere in a panorama of color, motion and sound. She is taken aback and must steel herself to continue out of the dark.

Off to the left, in the bustle, she sees a woman in a blue dress and red scarf turn to her. With a kind look she beckons Ana to come out. She takes her hand and pulls her behind the counter. "My dear, you look terrible. How do you feel? You took a hard fall. You have been sleeping for three days. We feared you would be joining your mother."

"She was not my mother; she was the mother of my betrothed. Do you know what has become of her?"

The woman turns her head to the ground and makes a sign with her first two fingers, then casts it over her shoulder. Taking a small pinch of something from under the counter she cast that over her other shoulder.

"We must not talk of the recently departed. She was placed in the ground yesterday while you were still feverish. She is with God now, so we should not call her back with this talk."

"Thank you. I am Ana, and I have not thanked you yet for your care. I have no way to repay you. Will you let me stay and help you until this debt is made right?" Ana's eyes water with the unshed tears of all that has happened. The woman, seeing this, takes her grief onto to her shoulders and lets Ana cry, holding her and gently rubbing her back. Passersby give the women none but a casual glance for this land has seen a lot of grief lately and seeing women crying has come to be a common sight.

Time passes and Ana, working hard, begins to understand more of the city and bustle she has placed herself in. Ionana and Lott, her husband, have taken her in. A strong bond grows between Ana and the older couple. They teach her what she needs to know to survive in the castle.

Ana works all day but in the early evening goes out into the night, seeking information and another sight of Cain. When she asks, Ionana tells her about the new nobleman who entered the castle a few weeks previous, and that he rented a house near the keep. Soon he was betrothed to the king's daughter, Iana.

This news comes as a shock to Ana and heavy does it set her heart to feel. She finds her way to the rented house and patiently sets herself to wait, hoping to catch a glimpse of this man who looks so like her love. Weeks pass and no glimpse, no whisper of sounds. The lights go on and off in the house and servants come and go, but she does not see this doppelganger of her once love.

She decides to be more direct. He must be staying in the keep. She knows that the princess is to be his bride so she seeks out the chamberlain for the king's staff. She does this by a small bribe to the woman who empties the night slops, she in turn whispers to the day mistress of the castle, who then speaks to the chamberlain.

He is a crafty man, gaunt and quick, with small darting eyes. His shoulders are pinched and craven, his back stooped, and his hanging arms, held before his chest, are like vulture wings.

He takes her in with those eyes. The leering way he looks at her body makes her skin crawl, his eyes darting to her breasts and then her hips. She wishes now she had taken her shawl and had covered herself better.

Ana takes his measure; she knows the type of man he is by the twitch of his eyes when they finally meet her own. She stands straighter and bears his scrutiny. Let him look, the bastard, there were men like him back in her village. They push around the girls, but she was a woman. She pushes back her shoulders and proudly raises her head.

He smirks, but backs a little. "What do you want? Why are you bothering me, woman?"

Remembering her quest she asks, "I am looking for a man who disappeared from my village. He was my love and I must find him!"

He curls his lip, "Why, are you carrying his child?"

"No," she answers, "We were engaged."

"Ran from you, did he?" he answers with a lecherous smile.

Ana glares him down.

"And I suppose he looks just like our new prince?"

Caught off guard Ana replies, "How do you know this?"

The man chuckles, "I thought so! You are Ana! Cain has been expecting you."

She is stunned. "He knows I am here?"

In control now the chamberlain replies, "He has known you were in the castle since he saw you on the street with the old woman."

With a simmering fire in her voice now she asks, "Does he know about his mother, the woman who was run down in the street?"

"Yes, and he is very interested in you meeting his new betrothed. Come with me!" With this the man turns on his heel and swiftly re-enters the keep. Pausing he ushers her inside.

She is brought to a small room overlooking the audience chamber. She sees down below her the king on his throne and before him, on their knees, Cain and a beautiful woman, who must be Iana, the king's daughter.

Iana is at first glance a beautiful woman, her hair golden blond, tall and fair skinned. Then Ana notes the slow way she moves, and other things about her, almost but not quite right.

Cain holds her hand. As Ana listens he asks the king to bless their union.

All at once everything she knows of Cain -- the image of him in her mind, the way he whispered her name in her ear when they sat under the old tree, the way he looked at her from the corner of his eyes, not daring to meet her eyes -- everything told her this was not Cain; this was a foul intruder in Cain's body.

But as she looks down on the great hall, the little things -- the way he holds his head, the tone of his voice, the little contained gestures his hands make as he speaks -- all of them tell her that the man pledging himself to this woman is indeed her Cain. It makes her want to scream, to take out her justified rage on him, the man she loves, the man who has forsaken her. At the same time she is baffled. Why would he do this?

Her mind races, she reaches out and takes the balcony's stone railing in her hands. Her knuckles whiten with the pressure as she tries to squeeze reason out of this, tries to find a logical explanation, to stop this mad rush toward insanity.

Words are exchanged between Cain and Iana, then between them and the king. Blessing and promises; this is the request blessing, the first step to a betrothal; they are to be married very soon.

Ana does not hear but her mind fills in the moments. She suddenly jumps to the wild conclusion that Cain may be insane. Could he have fallen, hurting his head and this other thing has arisen from her Cain... her Cain? Where did that come from? Was she already assuming that there were two Cains? Her Cain was this kind, generous woodcutter that would not talk to her loudly because he believed she would break. And this other Cain... who knew what he was capable of?

Then the sadness set in, tears cloud her sight, and the sound of her quiet sobs block out the world for a moment. She lowers her head and puts her forehead to the railing and mourns her breaking heart.

After the ceremony, Ana again composes herself. She notices the king has his councilor assist him down from his throne and he hobbles away out of the great hall, leaning heavily on the offered arm. So the rumors in the street were true, the king is not well.

In a few moments Cain appears on the balcony still dressed for the ceremony. He approaches her closely. She looks up to him with expectancy in her eyes. Many questions run through her mind but her emotions close her throat and her heart races in her chest. She feels caught between anger and sheer joy at his presence. All the things she had thought, all the experiences of the last few weeks roll back and forth through her mind. Prayers of thanks for his apparent good health and curses for his actions swing her from the point of tears to the point of rage.

She tries again for words. While trying to clear her throat she looks closely into his face and sees there something that again robs her of speech. There is only cold calculation in his eyes, no emotion of any kind. Ana is not prepared for this coldness. Cain had never been able to meet her eyes easily; his shyness had never let him face her full on. Now she is unprepared for the hardness of his eyes and the direct intensity of his demeanor. With her eyes she tries to reach beyond the icebergs to the man she knows is there, just out of reach. She can feel him; she knows he is there. But there is also a bleakness, a darkness on his heart. She tries but cannot reach him. Her failure deadens her own heart.

Past understanding the events that are carrying her along, no longer caring what happens to her, her own warmth dissipates, absorbed in the chill freeze of Cain's stare.

"I think she was trying to enter the keep, maybe to harm the king?" Cain's voice is rasping flakes of ice from the greater winter of his eyes.

The chamberlain answers crisply, "Yes, your majesty."

A smile forms from one side of Cain's mouth, twisting his face into a mask of ridicule.

Then as if a rope has tightened on his throat, he jerks and turns to the open rail. A distant look comes over his face. Down in the great hall, back in the shadows near the great arches that lead to the foyer, there is the barest hint of a smile from the vaguely female form. Her hand appears from her robes; thumb up, she slowly turns her hand. Cain's eyes go totally blank; as from a long way off his command is but a whisper. "Put her in the pit."

The chamberlain looks to this man, his soon to be new prince, and his blood runs cold. "Yes, your majesty."

The descent to the bowels of the keep takes but a blink for Ana. The spiraling stairs drill down; the stones become cooler and damper with each step. The walls narrow till Ana feels the weight of the castle settling on her shoulders. The realization of her situation does not sink in until she sees the pit itself. It cuts through her depression.

"No!!! I can't go there! Not down there!"

Then she notices the chamberlain is not with her anymore; somewhere along the way he was replaced by this creature. He walks with a limp and stagger. His face is a mass of scars and burns; his eyes dark pits in his head, one lower than the other; parts of his head covered by a shaggy mane of brown hair, the rest red skin, pimples and rash where he has scratched the hair off. His voice, when it comes, is half mad, mixed with at least three poorly learned languages. "Si! You will. Drop down jos. Way jos."

Ana hugs herself tightly, feeling the cold deep in her bones. Her face is drawn and white and she shakes; bone deep she shakes. Turning to run from this hole in the earth, she comes up against Cain.

"It is dark in the hole and it is very deep. You cannot see the bottom from here; the angle is too great. It takes a long time to put you down there. And it is not often that we bring someone up… It's easier to just forget that you are down there and leave you." The twisted look is on his face again and a gleam is in his eyes. His tongue traces his lips like he is savoring a favorite meal, each bite a taste of Ana's fear.

As the ropes are drawn and the creature approaches to tie them to her for the descent, an idea comes to her. "I will be her slave, Cain! I will be the princess's slave and I will take care of her!"

The distant look leaves his eyes; the twisted face is replaced for a moment with a glimmer of something. She sees it, but was it sympathy or something more sinister?

He holds his hand up for the creature to stop; it backs away. Ana is left with the cold of the pit at her back and the black emotionless void of Cain before her.

"Yes, you will do fine!" With this he takes her arm in his hand. Pushing her ahead, he sets her on the climb to the surface and daylight.

Chapter Four

Ana:

Cain takes her up through the keep, to the princess's tower. As she ascends, she begins to realize how all her dreams are so far away now. Her new world is painted all in dark colors. Everywhere she turns her choices are between death and pain. She remembers Ionana and the beautiful bright colors, the smooth cloths and bright stones of the market.

Her mind escapes back to when Cain held her in his arms and they had planned their wedding, how she had planned to make the most beautiful dress for her wedding, a dress like no other dress.

The Witch:

In the shadows, the witch grasps Ana's mind. She sees the dreams and latches onto the image of the dress. She smiles, a wicked thing to behold if anyone could see through the cloak of darkness she wears, and in that smile there is malevolent glee; this is exactly what she was looking for, the tool she can use to capture this soul.

Ana:

She beseeches Cain; their love before that night he disappeared. She remembers the quiet nights talking by the fire in her home and the quick and easy way he smiled. She remembers and smiles despite it all. She reaches out, almost touching him, with tears in her eyes and a dream-like quality to her voice.

"Do you remember any of it?" she asks, seeking with words for his lost soul.

"Do you remember me?" her voice breaks in a final effort.

Her words do find him, but not without a price.

Cain stops with his back to her. "I remember it all; all the time spent wasted in that small village while the real world was here. Wasting my life, when all the truly important things were happening here. But no more. I will have power and everyone will obey me or die." There is a timbre to his voice that hints of madness. There is fire in him. But the flames are cold, feeding off a bottomless pit of dementia.

His words fall like blows on her: repudiation of her people, her life trivial and a waste. This is not the person she knew, this is not her Cain.

She lowers her head now, her heart and body wilted; the life inside of her curls back on itself in pain. Her efforts to reach him are defeated. The small ship carrying her heart has crashed on the shore of his dementia, unable to reach the quiet welcoming dock that had sustained them for so long.

"Where have you gone, why are you so cold?" Ana speaks quietly to Cain's back not knowing what his response will be.

Cain turns to her, and with a calculated swing, he strikes her face.

"You will do what you are told and I will not throw you in the pit. Obey and I will let you live." His eyes are a dead wash of baleful displeasure.

The power of his strike is enough to spin her around and her face stings from the blow but she is more stunned than hurt that he struck her. She turns her face back to him, her blood boiling with the indignation and rage of being so treated.

Before she can strike out or even reply, their eyes meet and in that moment, that long forever moment, she is transported to a place of such cold and loneliness that the effect is immediate. It consumes her rage and consumes like a torch snuffed in the snow.

He turns his back to her again and continues walking. Her mind and soul now taken by the same cold distance that marks him, she follows, through the passages, and up through the tower to the princess's chambers.

The Witch:

Behind them, moving from shadow to shadow with an unearthly grace; chimerical as she flows from corner to corner, ghosting through passages and corridors as she passes servants, unseen, heading in the other direction. She puts a touch on each, tasting of their spirit, like a mendicant at a feast. Her mind uses the energy collected to feed the insanity of Ana, twisting her mind little by little, turning her mind with the madness love becomes as sanity leaves and mania seeds the will and soul with delusions.

Iana:

She is sitting in her rooms, taking off the combs and ribbons from the earlier ceremony, and thinking about Cain. Her thoughts of him have been in turmoil since they were introduced. His existence unknown just weeks before, now she finds an almost addictive need for him, this man of mystery from a distant land, here to save her and the kingdom from her father's imminent death.

It is amazing how he has gathered so much power to himself in such a short time. It is as though he has an angel over his shoulder lighting his way; he never hesitates or appears to doubt.

There is a knock at her door. She stands and Cain enters with a young woman. Her head is down so Iana cannot see her face.

"I bring you a gift," he says. The woman is sullen and will not look up to meet her eyes. "Her name is Ana." With this she lowers herself slightly in a curtsey.

Iana reaches out and lifts her chin with a finger. "She is beautiful, my love. Where did you find her?" She notices the little flinch in her face. 'There is a story here,' she thinks to herself.

"Oh, she came in off the street." He smiles slightly at this. It must be more of his cold twisted humor. The longer she knows him the less she actually likes her soon to be husband.

"I will return later; use her as you wish." With this he sweeps from the room, leaving Ana and Iana alone.

"Here girl, put my clothing and ribbons away." She indicates the piles on the chair and bed. Ana begins to fold and roll the ribbons, so quickly and carefully. The princess is amazed. Other servants and slaves she had would have taken hours for the simplest of tasks. She watches the way Ana handles the fine clothes and precious ribbons.

"Do you know how to sew and weave?" She looks down at Ana as she works, folding and packing the clothes.

"Yes." Ana does not meet her eyes; she keeps her face averted.

"Good, I will have much use for you." She smiles at Ana like a child with a new toy.

Ana:

That evening after many chores and much work one of the old women, who also serves the princess, shows Ana where she will be sleeping: a small room that serves as a seamstress's work room with a bed against the wall.

Exhaustion overtakes her as she goes to the bed.

In the dreams of Ana:

Evil whispers to her ear.

"IF she is alive she will SUFFER to see CAIN MARRIED with ANOTHER WOMAN. She will be NEAR HIM but NOT ALLOWED to TOUCH HIM or LOVE HIM. She will NEED to keep all this LOVE INSIDE. Better to DIE but CAIN IS SOO CRUEL! If she speaks out, or NOT OBEY he has the POWER to KILL HER with a glance."

She wakes once, the feeling of a presence with her, darkness by the door. But exhaustion takes her back before she is more than touching the surface of her conscious awareness.

"If she is ALIVE she will SUFFER. If she sees CAIN MARRIED with ANOTHER WOMAN she will have to KILL HIM!"

These dreams invade her, seeping in through her exhaustion, taking root in her sleeping mind, sowing the seeds of violence, as the shadow grows closer, reaching out to her.

Again she is back in the pit, shaking and cold to the bone. This time she is in the rope harness being lowered into the darkness, the ugly troll babbling as the warmth and light recede. Far beyond fear now her heart calms and out of the darkness she sees something. It is only a vague shape but it has a purpose that is just out of her reach; a power in doing what she needs. She struggles in the rope harness. She must do this and she feels that if she can do this, not all her dreams will be dead; one dream will remain, and though in her mind it is a clouded dream it is her only hope.

She wakes at dawn, the light of a new day just creeping under her door, not touching her within her dark chamber. She rises with hunger and the feeling that there is something she needs to do, but can not quite remember. She steps out of her small room into the lighter room, and there on a stool by her door is her gray raiment: the clothes of a slave.

Reaching down she takes the clothing and steps back into her room, her eyes full of tears. Memories of the previous day come crushing back on her like a wave of anxiety and she throws the dress to the floor. Focusing her anxiety and anger on the simple dress, she strikes out and kicks the offending piece of cloth across the room. Her eyes follow its flight as it lands in a heap against the wall.

Something catches her eye: a door. She must have been very tired last night to miss this. With the door open a crack, she notices within a covered shape with the glint of a mirror at the edge. A single step takes her to the door. Reaching with a tentative but curious hand she pulls the door open to reveal something very large covered in a heavy grey drape. She reaches out and touches the heavy covering.

Three things happen: the cover falls to the floor, there is a flash, and the mirror cracks.

Ana pulls her hand away as if stung; she jumps back and slams the door, her heart leaping to her throat. As the initial shock dissipates, she replays what just happened. Did she imagine the flash? Is the mirror really broken? Turning, she reaches out and takes the door handle. Holding her breath now she slowly pulls the door open and peeks into the dark space; she sees the mirror: a large thing in a heavy black wood frame. The frame is carved into the face of a fierce creature holding the glass in its mouth, the clear silver glass stretching the lips, and the four huge fangs frame whatever is seen there. Opening the door open further she is appalled to see the long dark crack running the length of the beautiful glass mirror. As she stares at her imperfect reflection her fears touch her heart with tendrils of apprehension. What will happen to her when Cain hears of this? How can she explain? It was her hand that touched the covering. Her fear deepens; she must think.

She picks up the heavy draping and covers the mirror. With it covered she feels strange, like she is not quite all there. She checks to see that she is alone in the room. She reaches out and lifts the edge of the drape; the reflection is of her own weary face. For some reason this makes her feel better. She folds the drape back and leaves the edge of mirror uncovered. Without thinking about it she kneels down on the floor before it.

Ana's eyes glaze over as her mind reaches into the mirror. Images and shapes dance before her, a mirage of shapes and shadows form, taking on substance and motion before her eyes: a long marble hallway, handsome men with beautiful women in lovely gowns on their arms, twirling and flowing around her as in a great dance, their graceful motions the image of perfection.

As she sinks deeper into the magic of the mirror Ana sees the shape and style of each gown, each one unique and lovelier than the last. And then she reaches the end of the hall.

At the top of white marble stairs, swirling and dancing to the unheard music, appears perfection in dressmaking. So rich and splendid, it appears as one piece of cloth: pure white silk alive in the sweep of its hem and trail, every motion of the wearer becomes a flourish and grand gesture of the gown.

The door slams in front of her, severing her from the mirror. Her mind is flung back into her skull. For only a moment it seemed she looked upon the glass.

Cain is there, looking down on her with his eyes flashing, one hand on the door, the other on an intricate dagger at his waist, cold steel and hand tense, and ready.

Ana falls to her side panting, out of breath; her eyes gritty, tongue swollen, legs and back sore as if from many hours of sitting tensely in that position. The whole episode in the mirror drifts away from her now, except the dress.

Cain takes her by the arm, draws her to her feet, then cruelly pushes her back to the closed door, his face inches from hers. Those dead eyes again consume her and she is lost in their frosted realm. She cannot scream as the cold leaches her strength and will, his hand ready with the dagger.

"Cain? Where are you?" Iana enters the room breaking the moment.

Cain slides the knife back, and allows Ana to escape his grip in a retreat away from him. Breathing hard and shaking, a brief respite allows her to realize with renewed terror that she is truly lost.

Jana:

Last night was very strange. After going to bed she did not sleep well and that she hates; it just ruins her day.

Now this! Another indication of history between her fiancé and this woman. Today she can see that she is a woman. Her eyes have a haggard cast to them that she had not noticed yesterday. Today she also notices how she looks at him: a combination of emotions pass over her face, like she loves him one moment and is terrified of him the next. He, on the other hand… not a flicker of emotion touches him, but that is how she has come to know him. The only emotion that ever crosses his face is that strange smile, so cruel and twisted. The memory makes her shiver; she is sure he has never looked at her that way.

Stepping between them, she says, "Take me for a walk in the garden?" and takes him by the arm. He nods, then leads her from the room.

Chapter Five

Ana:

*L*ater that day as she cares for the princess's wardrobe, washing, folding and inspecting every garment for damage, stains or wear, her mind goes back to that eternal moment in the mirror. The dress haunts her, twirling in her mind, each time building on what she had seen, adding details. Slowly she comes to believe she can make this dress.

When she has moved on to the great bedroom with the billowing drapes that protect the princess from drafts, she sees their shape as a shadow of the dress. By the time she lights the candles for the evening, everything has taken on the form of pieces of the gown. The candles even drip the wax in such a way that reminds her of the decorations along the hem.

The woman who showed her the way to her room the previous night sees her distraction and makes it a game to nudge or push things into her whenever she drifts away, thinking about the dress. Ana pays no attention to this but stops daydreaming just long enough to finish the chore of the moment. After awhile the woman gives up, but not before Ana has numerous minor cuts and bruises on her legs, back and arms.

At the end of the day she finds her way back to her little room. When she opens the door she notices there is a spinning wheel where the door used to be. She goes to it then notices it is no spindles for the yarn or thread. She walks around the wooden device… When she touches the wooden seat three things happen: there is a bright flash, the wheel begins to spin, and she finds herself sitting on the seat, her hands before her. With no wool for the wheel to spin, she does not know what to do. Then she notices another presence in the room with her. Her attention was distracted by the spinning wheel when she entered or she might have sensed the malignant presence that now pervades the small space; she might have had the chance to run away and save herself from what came next. But that time is gone.

The witch approaches the captive woman sitting on the seat of her trap. With tenderness that belies the malignancy of the deed she is about to subject Ana to, she reaches out and touches her beautiful black hair. She runs her hands down her soft cheek to a point right over the center of her chest where she touches Ana; with very little pressure she reaches into her chest! Her hand finds something there and with effort, her face straining and all but bursting with malignant glee, she pulls a little more and her hand exits Ana's chest, pulling along with it a thin gossamer thread. This thread is pure white and pulses warmly with the life of its source.

At the witch's first touch Ana's eyes lose focus; her mind retreats to the grand ballroom of the images from the mirror. She is now dancing with a faceless man. Upon the grand pedestal at the top of the marble stairs the dress glows and radiates its glory.

When the witch laces the thread through the collector guide and it snakes from Ana's chest onto the large wheel, she moans a little, feeling the drain of her life. The wheel takes the thread. Spinning faster and faster it collects the thin filament, while in front of Ana a wooden dress mannequin begins to glow with the outline of something.

Ana dances with the unknown man. Music is everywhere as she dances, her feet following the beat.

With every pulse, her eyes seek out the gown on the pedestal, seeing anew its sublime beauty and perfection. Her hands reach out to touch the soft, fine fibers of its weave.

All the while the terrible wheel spins her soul into the form that she sees and touches.

There is a sound at the door to her room; Cain is there. Without a word, a thought, or even a spark of abhorrence that any human being would have, he slowly pulls the door closed on his once love and the evil that is now feeding on her soul.

Ana:

Much later, as the dawn rises and the light of a new day reaches again under the crack of the closed door, she becomes aware. The dance in the ballroom reached a climax just before sunrise when the darkness was deepest and she had begun to feel tired; the first feeling she had had in the great ballroom other than the intoxicating draw of the gown. With the increasing fatigue comes the first double vision of awareness that she is in two places at once: she sees the spinning wheel and gown before her as a shadow overlaying the great hall that surrounds her. The great hall fades as the sun brightens and dawn's light illuminates her room, outlining the gown in stark white before her. As she sees the gown better, she also sees herself feeding the hungry wheel and can sense her soul unraveling into the terrible device. She would scream in terror if the awesome nature of what was being done to her did not take her will as well as her soul from her. The dress pulses and moves as it grows off the sustenance of her soul, focusing her attention, and she begins to see the resemblance to the dress of her vision. She would have broken then and torn the moment asunder with her screams and thrashing but the witch is there. She reaches out to Ana again and touches her forehead sending her once more into the world of the ballroom. The power of the gown again entrances her and she is once more blissfully unaware of what is being done to her.

Moment by moment more of her immortal soul is leached from her into the gown. Midday comes and there is a slight, hesitant knock at the door. The witch, focused on the process, is distracted for a moment, allowing Ana a brief return to awareness, her body racked and drained, showing her deterioration. Drained too many years past her physical age, she moans.

There is a startled exclamation as the handle is turned and the door is pushed slowly in, revealing the woman who the previous day had deliberately hurt Ana to try to keep her on task. As the light of the day streaks in revealing the tableau, shining light onto the horrendous plight of the woman on the spinning wheel, she covers her mouth and draws in the breath to scream. There is a blossoming of red on her chest as her body bends backwards. With the motion more blood is forced out as the blade itself is revealed between her breasts. Cain pulls back with a quick jerk and the woman falls into the room. Moving quickly, he closes the door behind himself.

The witch whispers to Cain and he drags the unlucky woman to where the mysterious closet door had been. The witch reaches to the wall and as she touches where the handle would have been the door is suddenly there. She backs away. Cain steps forward and draws the door open. Inside is a darkness as profound as darkest pitch is to midday shadow. He spins the once living maid around and, presenting her feet to the open door, begins pushing her through. Just as her feet disappear, she is suddenly ripped from him in a single motion. Snarling sounds, the ripping of flesh and cloth, followed by the breaking of bones comes from the darkness. There is no sign of emotion from Cain but the witch dances and jigs in glee to the mayhem and violence, soundlessly clapping her hands. In a moment the sounds stop. There is a slow exhalation of wind then a rather loud belch. The darkness lightens then slowly appearing from the dimness is the covered shadow of the mirror. Cain closes the door.

Ana hears this, but is unable to move, the power of the wheel and the witch hold her immobile as this horror plays out behind her back. Her eyes wide, the whites showing all around, she struggles to see behind her, to know the fate of the hapless maid.

All the while her soul feeds the wheel, relentlessly taking from her something she knows she cannot live without. Killing her; with a flow of her essence as thin as a thread.

She sees that the dress is half finished, a piece of knowledge she feels without knowing how she knows. She also knows that when it is done, if she is still alive, she will no longer be who she is. Pieces of her will and mind are like little stars inside the filament, details she was unaware of until that moment.

The witch, calming from her glee, turns to Ana and with a touch sends her away to the ballroom and time flows, taking Ana's life as her mind is elsewhere dazzled by the apparition she is creating.

Evening brings with it the darkening of the small room; Ana, returning to awareness again, feels the hours she has been gone, each leaving her less and less attached to this world, lighter of mind and less substantial of heart. She feels less, each moment taking away the cares of her life. With the cares go the memories of her family and friends. The feelings of sorrow and the feelings of joy all drift from her. In this great chasm of missing emotions and feelings is drawn at first simple basic needs, but behind them, as the opening space allows it, are other things, things alien to her soul, things that would corrupt and spoil her life if allowed to take root. The ability to fight those feelings, even the will to oppose the changes wrought within her is part of the silvery silk that is the essence of the gown forming before her eyes. As the changes begin, the flow of thread slows, each inch pulling its way from her, wrenching out like a piece of her body, jerking her and wrenching her physically now. Her body fights to hold onto the last of the goodness it has in sheer desperation. Her hands rise up and take hold of the thread, bleeding as it slices through them like wire.

The wheel strains now to keep up the progress of thread, fighting back with ever increasing power; there is a moment in time as the pull of her last strength and the pull of the wheel match. In that moment the tenuous fiber strains, then with a great flash and thunderclap of sound, rattling and shaking the tower, the thread breaks, rebounding back to Ana and throwing her backward to the wall.

The witch:

Stunned by the blast, her power slips and she is visible for just an instant. Then she is again transparent and a part of the shadow. If Ana had been conscious for that split second, she would have seen the twisted form; evil such as the eye cannot stand to look upon. But beneath that she would have seen a woman of Ana's apparent age and size with shoulder length black hair curled and floating around a beautiful face.

A moment passes then Cain is there at the door, looking upon the room. Shutting the door, he crosses to the candle on the small table beside the bed. Striking a spark he lights it and turns.

The spinning wheel is gone; the space it occupied is now empty. Deep burns on the floor mark out the places each leg had touched.

The gown: if there was any magic on earth that could have touched his soul it would have been this sight. Hidden from his eyes until now by the witch's glamour, it stands revealed to him. Pure white gossamer-thin lace borders shining white silk, sparkling in the candlelight like a beacon in the otherwise dark room. The beauty of this dress reaches into the land of fairy to touch the eye with things ethereal. It shimmers with a purity and life of its own.

Motion draws his eyes to the corner where Ana lies in a heap, thrown back against the wall and dazed. Making mewling sounds as she comes to, she pulls her legs up tight, into a fetal position; with eyes open, she scans the room.

Still dazed and disoriented but already the physical changes are very apparent to the woman returning to consciousness. The woman looking about the room is not Ana, or at least not the Ana who loved Cain; this creature is of another hue. Her face is now twisted and sour, her eyes squinted and untrusting. Her heart is cold and bitter, the last of the goodness guarded and hoarded like a merchant's purse. She looks up at Cain. There is no love now in that glare, just fear and loathing.

The witch in her corner cackles with glee.

Cain goes to Ana and reaches down as if to take her arm; Ana strikes out with her nails and a feral hiss escapes her clenched teeth. Cain draws back quickly and withdraws to the door as she looks about the room for something to throw.

When he leaves and closes the door, the witch also exits, sliding effortlessly out of the space, all but bursting with glee at the outcome of this phase of her plan.

Ana:

Hunched over with her fingers curled into claws she slinks to her bed. There she sinks into a dark place, thoughts of despair and vengeance mixed with self-loathing and the embers of something far worse.

No longer the bright wholesome daughter, nor the young woman so interested in life and living, she is now less than she was, and in that lessening she is released from the rules she had once sought to focus her life on. In her eyes now a thing takes root. This thing is neither human nor animal for even an animal is restricted by the limits of its condition. With the small shred of her soul held close, an injured thing in tatters, the evil that is in all people has been released of the constrictions that her previously bountiful soul put upon it. She is free in a way all wraiths are free; without a conscience. Every slight, every hurt becomes a call for murderous retribution. Cain calls to her.

The Witch:

With a smile on her face, hidden within her magic, she shadows Cain as he makes his final preparations for tonight. The king, succumbing to his illness, has settled into a very deep sleep that is thought he will never awaken from. Cain is in control through his relationship with the princess. All that is left is the wedding, and now that the dress is done, she will control the princess like she has Cain. How could the princess not crave the beautiful thing? How could she not want to trade her soul for it?

The things she will have them do for her, the pain she will put the people through, and the hardship. What fun! Passing a servant in the hall she reaches out and takes a taste of the woman's misery; it is a draft of sweetest nectar to her. Oh, how she will feast.

Ana:

She rises from her bed. She moves now in a fluid half crouch, hunching her back. Pulling a blanket with her she ties it in a cowl thus allowing her to hide beneath its covering mass. She approaches the door. Unlocked she turns the knob.

In the hallway the torches in the main halls feel threatening to her; light is no longer her friend. She makes for the side corridors. Slinking from darkness to darkness, she bears a strange resemblance to the witch as she stalks the upper halls of the castle.

Inside her mind a war wages. Every moment insanity rages as the fragmented pieces of her fight for control. The darkness which has filled her works for the ends of her tormentor; the need for blood and the release of pain are all palpable as sweet meats to her tongue.

There is another part of Ana that still lives though greatly diminished. It cries out; it feels all the pains done to her. This part knows what she is doing is wrong. This part still loves and would do what is right. This part remembers the warmth of the sun.

The thoughts flow through the tortured, hunched body like liquid fire, twitching her frame and starting and stopping her movement. If any could see beneath her hood they would be sure of the insanity of this creature, if not its identity.

At the turning to the hall that leads to Cain's suite of rooms she falls to her knees. Her hands reach to her face and the good within her makes its first stand. Images of a better place and better times flood her mind. From seeds of beauty spring images of her favorite flower, the warmth of the fire on the dark winter nights at home, petting the thick wool of the sheep and feeling that same wool flow through her fingers as she spins…

This image is suddenly replaced by the image of the spinning wheel in her room that has stolen her soul and taken her comfort, joys and memories. With this the pain racks her and again she is in motion, murderous thoughts warp her once beautiful face into a hideous death mask of fury and revenge.

Taking the turn and entering the hallway, she lurches forward. At the first door she hears voices, not of Cain but of the chamberlain and a woman. She passes this door and approaches the second door on the same side of the hallway. There is no sound but she perceives with an almost animal sense the radiation of malignance, the feeling of foreboding that seems to follow Cain but does not seem to emanate from him. She turns from the door and crosses the hall.

As she puts her hand on the ornate handle she is certain. This is where he is; this is Cain's room. The metal handle is cold in her hand as she hesitates for a second, letting her senses reach into the room, feeling for him or for anything that would get in her way. She slowly pushes the door in to the room.

The sitting room is small in comparison to the room that lies beyond, with ornate furniture arranged in perfection, untouched and static. She slides into the room and pulls the door silently closed behind her.

Then she sees it! Casually cast aside, the only thing out of place, on a table outside the door to his bedroom where he must be sleeping now. She approaches it with a gleam in her eyes. This is what she was hoping to find, a tool for her evil tonight: Cain's dagger.

Something rises in Ana at the sight of the dagger, some deep primal thing that lives off blood and gore. This thing comes forward to the front of her mind taking control. It snatches the sharp gleaming dagger from the table and holds it to the weak moonlight; softly touching it, runs a thumb from base to tip, testing the sharp edge. A start comes from her as the blade draws blood from her already ravaged fingertips, gouged bloody from the ordeal with the spinning wheel. She puts the finger tip to her mouth and tastes blood.

Still in command this entity turns Ana to face the door to Cain's bedroom. The dagger is now turned point down to stab, hilt in her hand.

She finds the door unlocked as she moves forward and without a sound she is inside his bedroom. In the darkness she seeks out the form of a man lying upon the bed   sleeping, a dark colored dressing gown at the foot of the bed. 'Perfect,' she thinks as she goes around to the side of the bed. She positions herself to the side of the bed closest to him. He is on his back and Ana can clearly see his breathing body before her laid out as if in sacrifice.

There is a moment before thought becomes action, before the will exerts final control over the body; an opportunity Ana's good half could not surrender.

Images of her family come to her; the quiet times in their home around the table laughing together. Her eyes fill with tears that wash down her face.

Overlaying those images is the episode in the depth of the castle where Cain threatened to throw her down the well. Her face hardens and the tears of loss turn to those of anger.

Sounds assail her: the remembered laughter and the cries of her little brother when she would tickle him and play with him in the summer grass. Her face melts and her chest begins to loosen with the coming sobs.

The sounds turn to the clatter of hooves on the cobbles, the small cry as Cain's own mother was crushed beneath the hooves of his charging horse. Her mouth stiffens to a cold white line.

In this immortal conflict she is poised above Cain, his heart calling to the knife in her hands. The beast within her presses her tenuous hold upon the plunging knife while the soul of goodness, diminished by the workings of the evil witch's magic, struggles to build itself within the breast of a pure good woman, unused to the sway of evil.

One final chance is left for her. She hears Cain's voice telling her of his eternal love; she smells his sweat after a hard day of work; she sees him descending the mountain road with his hat laid back on his head, smiling as he sees her across the field.

The demon throws images of him from the ceremony in the great hall, the feelings of cold from his eyes. But these are things that he also was a victim of, and his soul and the person within were not there; she knows this now.

One final image: It was a cool day in the fall. She was cold because she had left her warm shawl in the house. She had gone to the church to deliver some food and was walking home. Cain caught up to her from behind and had seen her shiver holding her arms to her chest. He opened his warm cloak and enfolded her in a hug, his warmth taking her by surprise. She turned to him and in that moment eye to eye, close and warm with her love, she had melted in his arms. Wrapping her arms around him she had reached for him and they kissed.

With this memory her soul feeds, for in love there is much sustenance for a weary heart. With a strength she cannot fathom she attacks the demon in her body, striking with a will and power restored by the sure knowledge of a once great and lasting love that would be again, though it takes a century. The demon, tasting its defeat in the swelling of the presence kept so tightly away from its grasp, searches for an escape.

The knife begins to glow malignant green in her hand.

In the darkened room Cain, unaware of the immanent doom hanging above his heart, sleeps on.

With pathways of power open to her now, Ana goes after the demon. In this immortal moment within her mind she has won the battle and her foe has retreated, but his bastion lies still within her grasp. With the power bursting now from its seed, her love for Cain powers her intent as her mind reaches out to the offending tool of murder in her hand.

Three things happen all at once: A flash of the most pure white lights blazes out, lighting up the room for an instant; a spark so bright the night watch takes it for a lightning strike, but as there are no clouds, let alone a storm, they keep their thoughts to themselves and no report is made. The glowing knife disappears in that flash. And in its place is the most perfect crystal rose.

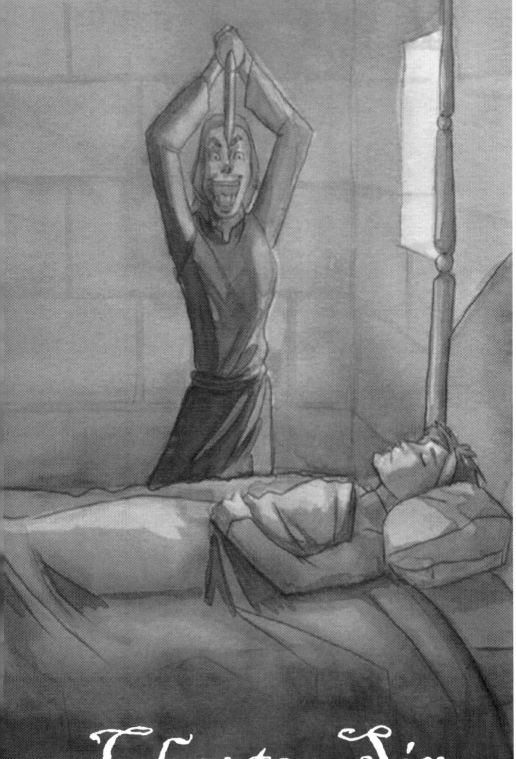

Chapter Six

Ana:

There is no time for her to hesitate. The cover of darkness will soon be replaced with the dawn's rays and she must disappear long before then. Holding close her prize she scurries from his room. Cain sleeps on, unaware of the nearness of his own death, a passing of the grim reaper of souls. She must escape the castle and its walls before morning. She has much to do and very little time.

When she gets to the door she stops for a moment, testing the air and listening for sounds in the corridor. She knows the nature now of the threat and the true prison he endures. She also understands what has been done to her and where she must go, if she can, and if she is strong enough.

She glides down the corridors looking for the door that leads to the kitchens of the keep; it has been days since she last ate or drank anything. The thought of food pushes her faster. She is painfully aware of that passed time. It has aged her far beyond her time, she is no longer young nor beautiful but she is herself once again.

At the stairs she pauses again, searching with all her senses. There is something wrong here but she can't quite place it; a presence draws near. She picks a door and silently draws it open: a linen niche. She enters and pulls the door closed, peeking out the crack she leaves in the door.

A shadow from the torches in the hall shows her someone walking down the hall. As the shadow approaches she sees nothing attached to it; it is alone on the floor like a loose dog padding along without its master. She gasps to herself, drawing back from the doorway, fearing not only the shadow but the elusive master.

She waits until she is sure the shadow is gone then quietly continues her descent into the keep, following her nose. Sure that the kitchens will be busy at this early hour, she is hopeful of some warm bread and maybe meat. She finds the kitchen, off the main corridor at the back of the keep on the ground floor. As she approaches the door the bustling sounds and the smells of baking bread and cooking meat make her head reel and her mouth water. She walks in boldly knowing any hesitation would tell the cooks that she does not belong; she is there to get her mistress an early morning breakfast, no more. Upon entering the kitchen she is shocked to find the trollish man from the dungeon. He leans against the wall, carelessly chewing bites from a loaf of bread and drinking a cup of tea, talking between bites with one of the bakers as old friends might.

With eyes wide she shuffles forward to the cook. Catching his eye he asks, "Hello, mother, what can we get for you?" Her eyes go even wider but she is able to squeak out her cover story with a minimum of starts and stops, not realizing just how weak she is until she had to speak. The baker listens carefully, and then with a turn, is gone into the kitchen to fill her order.

The troll turns to look at her. Listening carefully, she can just understand his jabbering speech. "Who are you?" he asks. She answers that she is the servant of the princess. He asks again who she is. She answers, "I am no one; you do not know me." With this she turns from him, placing a stone pillar between them trying to end their conversation. He pursues her. Taking his tea and the last of the bread he circles the pillar and stands before her. She thinks he asks her what she does but is unsure of her interpretation and is saved from answering by the return of the baker carrying a heavily laden basket of bread, meats and a crockery pot of steaming tea. She takes the basket and turns to the door. He is there, before her, blocking her way.

The cook sees this and rounds the counter to confront him. In a mix of languages not unlike the troll's he asks him why he stops this woman. The troll replies and the two men continue speaking. Ana's mouth waters and she swallows the flood of saliva as she stands smelling the fresh food, literally starving. The cook turns to her and explains, "He is a good man but he is not always right in the head. He says he remembers you from the dungeon but that you were much younger then. He wants to know what happened for you to become so old in a week." The cook looks to Ana, his eyes expecting her to laugh so he can brush it off as ravings. Ana looks past the cook and locks eyes with the troll. She says one word, then pushes past the men and is out and down the corridor heading for the main hall. After that the east door that leads to the street -- the same door she entered the keep, so many years ago, only last week.

Dawn is touching the land with the lambent fingers of stark discovery when she exits the small door in the stone wall and is again in the open air. Her small exhalation of relief is all the celebration she allows herself as she walks rapidly down the street. With her burden in her arms before her, her goal is the east gate, the closest to the keep.

The guard on duty is only just awake; groggy, he opens the massive iron and wood gate then the portcullis with a grunt.

With a sigh of relief she descends the path from the castle and is half a league from the gate before she turns off the road and enters the forest. Finding a large tree with a shady place between its roots she settles down and lets herself relax, opening the basket. She knows that she cannot eat all the food; she does not want to get sick and lose her hard won meal. She leaves more than half for later.

As she sips the tea her hands begin to shake. She sets the small cup down and all that has happened to her over the last few days hits her like a brick; she surrenders to the anguish of her ordeal. Sobbing and crying she covers her face with her hands. It is a long time before the sobs abate to the deep breathing of exhausted sleep.

Eyes from the forest watch her sleeping form, yellow eyes with the cold hard stare of predators stalking prey. Creeping on silent pads ever closer to the motionless woman, the fox is after the basket of food still clutched close to her chest. Out into the open shadow of the great tree it stalks, sniffing as it moves forward, wary of the least motion or sound. A few inches from her it pauses, ears uplifted and its whole body suspended as it is but a moment from its goal.

There is a whistling sigh as the arrow takes the animal in its heart, thrown back in startled and sudden death.

In a moment, another figure emerges from the forest; this one crouched over, the nocked arrow ready, bow held point down as he approaches his sleeping sister. Lupul takes the basket from her sleeping form and with sure deft motions he lifts her from the roots of the tree, across one shoulder. Approaching the dead fox he puts the limp body with his other kills in the bag hanging from his belt. He is careful not to leave any evidence of his or her presence as he backs out of the shadow of the great tree into the deeper forest.

It is early dawn the next day before there is any sign of life from the woman now covered by a warm blanket, reclined against the wall of a dark but dry and not unpleasant cave. She stirs and opening her eyes for a moment creaks out one word: "Water!" He brings her the mouth of the water skin and she drinks. Her eyes see then the shape before her and she knows him.

Iana:

She is sleeping soundly when one of her handmaids comes to the bedside whispering to wake her, urgency in her voice, "Wake my princess! It's the king; you must go quickly, my lady!" She turns and dreading the worst allows the maid to help her get dressed and made presentable. As the last button is done she exits the bedroom into her suite's sitting room.

Waiting for her, dressed for battle, are four guards and Cain. He greets her with a terse, "Iana, we must hurry to your father's room. He is very bad, and the physician says he is very near death."

She looks into his eyes: still no hint there of any feelings. Once again she wonders at her feelings for this cold man. 'Later,' she thinks. 'I will have time later to think about this. I must go to my father.' She brushes past the guards and takes his arm; she quietly and quickly allows Cain to take her from the room.

Occupying the east tower, the king's suite is an array of rooms; at the far east of these lies the bedroom. They approach the enormous double wooden doors.

Guards on each door, at the arrival of the princess, come to attention. Seeing she is escorted by Chancellor Cain they salute before opening the doors for the party. The princess's escort fall off to the sides and take up station with the king's guard.

All these men charged with diligence to protect both the dying king and the soon-to-be queen do not notice the extra shadow or the cold draft following the party through the open doors.

In the great bed, propped up on many pillows, lies an old man. Without the finery and stern demeanor all that is left is this simple small person, withered with age and infirmities.

The once great king, fighting the final battle of his life, now comes to the end of his power. The last of his great dreams is the simple wish to be among his loved ones and to come to the end of it quickly.

He opens his eyes at the approach of the company; they fall on his beautiful daughter, a tear in her eye and her hands out to take his outstretched grasp. She is there with him, holding and kissing his hand, dropping to her knees. Above her, his eyes take in the visage of Cain, impervious and imperial.

For a moment the king forgets who this cold, lean man is with his daughter and is ready to call the guards. Then the moment passes and he is once again looking into the eyes of his greatly trusted chancellor; confusion abates.

The king arches his back in pain at the cold presence that crashes into him, followed by a racking pain in his chest; he falls back gasping for breath. The physician comes forward to administer to the king. After a moment he retreats, shaking his head; these attacks have happened before. It will pass or not; no medicine he has can diminish the torment.

The king reaches out once more to hold his daughter's hand. He breathes slower and squeezes her hand reassuringly. With some final reserve of strength, he again opens his eyes.

Maybe it was his nearness to death or maybe it was an evil taunting of the witch that allowed the glamour to pass from his eyes for his final seconds, but for whatever reason, he sees his tormentor for the first time, lying in bed with him like a lover, her face inches from his, sucking the last of his life directly from his gasping mouth. Unable to utter a word, his face contorted in terror and abhorrence, the great king dies in a frantic moment of agony. There is nothing left but a husk of lifeless meat.

Ana:

It is time, she knows: the moon is right and she is ready. He will be here tonight. She and Lupul sit in a camp under the great oak just as the shadows lengthen into coming night. The fire is small, smokeless, and the tea is hot.

As the last of the day's embers glow and fade, then are squelched under the boot of approaching night, a form separates from the rest of the lengthening shadows. Circling the tree from behind, it takes a seat across from Ana.

The old man is as she remembers him. He pushes his face forward at her, in accusation. She recoils a little, his predictions hitting her with the strength of the slap that was never launched.

"What is your first question?" He picks up the cup from its place on a stick near the fire and fills it with the hot tea. Sitting back against the boles of the roots, he groans and settles back.

Lupul flares his nostrils testing the air but is still unable to smell anything to justify what his eyes tells him sits a meter away.

She looks across the fire, her eyes taking on a calculating quality; she reviews the questions in her mind, bringing to the front her first priority.

"How can I save him?"

His response is to sip the hot tea loudly. Then through lidded countenance, like a cat playing with a cornered mouse, he says, "That is a complicated question. Three things need to happen to save your Cain: he must be separated from the witch, she must release him, and you must also release him. To save him you must let him go!"

Stricken, she stiffens. No greater evil could he have done to her than this ultimatum. To save him she must let him go. So easy and yet the most fearful thing she can imagine. Stunned, she drops her tea. Hands shaking, she reaches for the cup; she cannot let her feelings touch her yet, there will be time for that later. For now she must focus on this being. Two more questions.

She stiffens, then reaching down with firmer hands she takes up her tea cup. He is there beside her pouring tea into her cup. No motion was needed for this; he was just there, then back across the fire, apparently never having moved, his stunning speed uncommented on. The tea, still warm, wets her dry throat.

"So, that is one. Now you have two more and the night grows old awaiting your pleasure." He snickers at his own wit as he settles back and takes another sip of tea.

Ana looks over to Lupul; he never shifts his stare from the old man as he reaches out to give her support, touching her shoulder, like her father did to encourage her.

"How can I undo what has been done to me?"

She lowers her head, uncertain how he will react to her apparent self-centered request, but he sees to her true question and answers, "There is a relationship between you, the dress and the witch!" She recoils at this and shakes her head at the possibility that she might be like or connected to that foul being. "You have to accept this and feel the path very carefully. There is a balance here and that balance is in the form of a very intricate dance, a dance between you and her. You must find your way out of this dance." He takes another sip of the tea. "The dress is pure and is but a tool to her. You must fight fire with fire." With this he looks down at the folds of her apron, in the pocket of which she carries the crystal rose; the prison of a demon. "The tool has to be destroyed for you to be whole."

She looks haggard and sick at the prospect of the future, the weight of which crushes her harder than the seeming weight of all the great mountains around her.

"Ahh, that was two, now you have but one question. You do age the darkness with your prattle. Get to it, woman, one left. Can't you see dawn approaches?"

Unimpressed with his antics, Ana casts no eye to the east. The last question; she has spent the two days since she escaped from the castle mulling this over. She is a very moral woman and the idea of what she asks may not be within her to carry out, but the memory of all that has happened to her over the last season pushes her to a decision.

"How can I kill the witch?"

Jana:

What a beautiful dress, she has never seen its like before. It shines like silver so pure and bright but is so soft she could touch it and stroke it forever. Even the lace is smooth and warm to her hand. Cain gave it to her; he just came in and handed her the dress. Not for the first time she asks herself how she can love such a cold man. The thought flits from her mind like a butterfly as she strokes the beautiful dress.

Last night she had such a strange dream: she was standing in a room and a strange woman was asking her to make a decision. She had a small red rose in her hand. She also had the dress. The woman told her she could have the dress forever as her own if she would take the rose. She had liked the rose; she saw no reason to not take both the dress and the rose, and the white dress would look very nice with the rose. She remembers reaching out for the rose and taking it from the woman who then laughed strangely. She knows the rest of the dream was a dream because what happened next could only have been a very bad dream. She remembers the rose had a thorn. When she took the rose, it pricked her. She tried to drop the rose but it stuck to her hand. She shook it to dislodge the persistent plant but it did not move. The rose seemed to take root in her hand, sinking the thorn deeper and deeper, until it seemed to be living off her blood. Then she reached out for the dress, the rose in control of her hand. The head of the rose stretched from her hand and seemed to slide atop the wonderful gown, crawling like a snake on a tree. Settling in place over the right shoulder it continued to extend its roots, pulling strength from her as it grew, and spread to accent the perfect gown with a green vine, the head of the rose spreading on the shoulder, becoming a complementary design. She fainted in her dream then and was soon awake in her bed; just a bad dream.

Then, today, she sees the lovely dress… with the green and red design.

Another butterfly of an idea flutters around her mind looking for escape. The witch chortles and dances around the room.

Cain:

'Here,' he thinks to himself as he stops in the small village a day's ride from the castle. He holds his hand up for his troupe of men to stop. They spread out around him facing the people coming out of their homes to see. He reaches into his saddle bag and takes out the rolled parchment.

"People of this town, I am Chancellor Cain, soon to be king. I come here to tell you there will be a new tax to build an army. This is necessary due to the encroachment of the kingdoms of the west who seek to take our lands and have killed many of our people. They think we are weak because we no longer have a strong king. We are going to teach them their mistake." With this he takes another document out of its case on his saddle and hands it to the soldier on his right who then rides forward. Dismounting, he nails the missive to the door of the church in the center of the village.

Turning his mount, Cain leaves the town, surrounded by his men.

Ana:

The sun is warm on her as she sits beside the well, just another woman enjoying the sun. She looks up from her bench. A young woman on the balcony is looking out over the kingdom; the new queen. She is very unsettled and for good reason: today is her wedding and her soon to be king has not returned yet from recruiting. Rumors abound of the hostility he faces in the country. All over the keep people talk of the pending war.

Ana slips from her seat as the queen turns from her perch and re-enters the keep. Slipping through the entrance into the main keep, Ana has a mission: she has to find the dress. Today is the wedding and today she has just one chance to stop the evil she is part of and recapture part of her soul.

As she walks through the keep she notices the changes since the last time she was there. Crowds of women decorate the halls with fresh blossoms and brightly colored drapes and decorations. She blends into the crowds and works her way to the queen's suite of rooms. She must get close to Iana to carry out the old man's instructions. She must do this before the wedding, before this evil can spread.

She carries a large armload of rushes up the stairs hiding her face and giving no reason for anyone to notice her. On the second floor, on edge now, she approaches the room of her capture and torture. She must find out if it is still there, or if the room is empty as she fears it may be. Opening the small door carefully she slips in, closing it behind her. Quiet and tense in her apprehension, she feels nothing as she looks over the room; she feels that this is just an empty room now. Going to the back wall from the door she puts her hands out touching the wall where the door had been, feeling for the evil that had inhabited this room. Turning, she leaves the room. The darkness that had touched her she can now leave behind.

She goes to the east seeking the old king's chambers. In the great hallway she walks with her arms loaded with blankets, a quick steady walk imitating the other women working for the wedding.

At the entrance to the king's chambers she stops; she feels something here. As she reaches for the great door handles she hears a voice behind the door. She sets her burden down on the floor and pretends to fold the blankets again, peering into the keyhole.

At first she only sees the closed drapes of the sleeping chamber. Letting her eyes follow the sounds, she looks to the left of the great bed. There is a shifting of the shadows, and a figure can be seen outlined in contrast to the streaks of light leaking in through the gaps in the curtains, a feminine form. Ana watches as the shape dances around the bed; quiet laughter can also be heard.

In horror Ana clutches the blankets to her chest and backs from the door; the witch is there and she needs more time to do her task before she can be discovered. Quickly now, her footsteps scuffing the stones of the floor in her haste, she goes west to the other end of the keep and the queen's chambers.

This is the center of the bustling activity and where she must go. She has to find the queen before she dons the dress.

Cain:

Riding hard, troops at his side, he approaches the keep. All night he has ridden to be here by day for his wedding. Two horses died beneath him and a third one will not survive this day. He does not care. He must be there and he will be, regardless the cost. He can see the castle over the next rise. His face twists into that callous half smile; he will be there on time to claim his bride.

At the base of the road ascending to the keep his horse gives out and with a final gasp drops to its knees and slides to a stop. He rises from the dead animal. Pointing to one of his troops he has the smaller man dismount, and then takes the soldier's mount. Putting heels to the animal, he races up the steep incline toward the east gate.

Having seen him from the walls the watch signals the main keep. Cain's valet is waiting with a stable boy to take his mount as he enters the keep.

He dismounts and quickly trots up to his new rooms in the east tower: the king's chambers.

Jana:

In her chambers, the queen hears of his arrival. The wedding is on then. She begins the long process of dressing for her ceremony: the slips and undergarments, the bows and pins for her hair. An older serving woman approaches her and with deft fingers weaves a very beautiful, tiny crystal rose into her hair. She looks in the mirror and for an instant thinks she recognizes the woman. The moment passes. The woman looks away and is gone, replaced by other maids with brushes and ribbons and other jewels. She forgets her and is again anxious for the ceremony to come.

The dress is brought in, carried with reverence in the arms of her favorite servant. The woman carefully lifts the gown to slip over Iana's head. As the dress descends over her head, she feels a coldness of heart descending like a shroud over her body; a shroud over her dead soul. The dress settles and much to the delight of the women dressing her seems to be custom fit to her body. Its sheerness and silken gloss beg the women to touch it and caress its silken loveliness.

Then something strange happens; the blood red rose on her shoulder moves, just a little, and she almost shrieks out as pain strikes her shoulder, going straight to her heart. There is a slight pressure from the red weavings like a snake tightening on its victim, settling in to crush the life from its prey. She gasps and staggers a little. Looking into the mirror she lifts the shoulder of the gown a little but sees no bloody root sinking through her shoulder into her heart. She looks into the mirror and sees only herself in the most beautiful gown she has ever seen looking back.

Cain:

The witch dances around him, cackling and clapping her hands. He sees her now as a misty form leaving her shadow a step or two behind her. Occasionally she turns mid-stride to capture and swing it like a dance partner.

He stands still as a statue, his garments melting from him. His body, cleaned by a hundred shadow hands and then dressed in blues and gold, is the image in the orb, right down to the ermine robe of the king. The promise fulfilled, as she said.

He looks into the great mirror of the old king and sees his reflection.

There is a timeless moment in the mirror; an old man, the king beyond the reach of death, stands from the bed behind him. He approaches and puts his hand on Cain's shoulder. His lips move and there are words; Cain cannot hear them but their meaning is plain on his face. The reflection of Cain in the mirror turns and takes the old man in his arms and hugs him as a son to a father. Then he turns back; the face now is that of the old Cain. Deep pain and misery have eroded his once handsome countenance, but there is joy and humor there as well, gone in a flash as the witch's dancing shadows cross his view.

Jana:

She crosses the great hall from the stairs, in slow cadence, to the north entrance of the keep with its double doors. Cain will meet her there and together they will take the twelve descending steps outside, cross the courtyard to the church, and then mount the church steps. Once in the church they shall be wed.

A great crowd is present to witness the joining. Cain is there to meet her at the great door. She takes his arm as the great doors are opened to the day and the waiting crowd. Great cheering greets the couple as they exit the keep.

As the day's full shine falls upon the dress and the crystal rose in her hair, three things happen all at once: a bright flash, the rose vanishes, and the red rose embroidery disappears in a flash of red fire that burns fast and hot, leaving the dress unmarred.

Then a shriek is heard; a sound of renting fury and anger. Not from any human does that sound arise. Silence falls over the courtyard as the queen staggers. Unhampered by the witch's glamour for the first time she looks around her and sees: Cain and all the past things she had seen but not seen, her father's death, a thousand things that she had seen but had not been able to react to or remember. She cries out again, this time in revulsion to Cain's arm in hers. She pushes him away.

The crowd, reacting to her anger and revulsion, has a moment of clarity allowing them to see through the witch's glamour. They direct their angry response to Cain, the man taking their queen. From somewhere in the mass comes a stone, striking short on the steps before him, then another. Lifting his arm he signals for the guard to enter the crowd. This is met with a surge of the masses toward the steps. More rocks are thrown and a piece of paving strikes Cain on the head; he goes down like the stone that struck him.

Ana is there, at his side. She takes his arm and helps him to the shelter of the door, back into the keep.

The witch is there too. She directs the anger and fear in the crowd like a conductor directing a band of musicians, insane glee on her face, feeding on the frenzy of violence. Using her craft to increase the negative nature of the crowd, surging it back then forward like a great wave, she swings it around the courtyard. Then, raising her arms, she collects and holds their emotions, drawing them deep into herself. Filling to bursting with the anger and fear, she finally sends them crashing back down into the crowd.

A wave of broken stone and rocks fall on the queen, destroying her. The gown is ripped to tatters.

Ana takes Cain to the east exit. Meeting Lupul there she hands off the limp body. He is secreted into a cart with the small pony, Stony, at its lead. They are away in a moment; none notice.

Sanity returns to the mob with the fall of the last rock. A cry then a shriek comes from a woman in the front, clutching her face, tearing at her apron, appalled at the depth of what has been done today.

The queen is dead.

Chapter Seven

Ana:

There is a peace that comes with the simple act of walking and listening to the play of squirrels in the quiet of the forest.

Two days have passed since they turned their backs on the castle; two days of worry. Would they be chased down? Would the guard want them back? There is no doubt that the burden they carry under the old blanket would be hunted. She also has no doubt that the witch is out there but as long as they keep moving there is a chance they will be able to get him to a place of safety in the mountains before she comes for him. Three more days.

This evening as she and Lupul sit on the roots of an old beech tree, staring into the glowing embers of the small fire between them, her mind returns to the faces of the crowd right before they slew the queen; she shivers. This is the nature of the power that is on their trail, seeking its marked prey.

She lifts her eyes to the dark form of her brother who sits unnaturally quiet and relaxed, an arm's reach from her, and wonders at the changes in him.

She clears her throat and for the first time in what seems days she speaks. "My brother, what has happened to you?" Her words reach across the fire as a rope crosses a chasm seeking the far edge and a stable hold.

His nostrils flare, as though scenting her words rather than hearing them. His voice, also raspy and low from lack of use, travels back on that same tether. "I have no words." With this his eyes touch hers; there is a fire in them and a weariness that had not been there before.

His face has also changed: leaner and stronger; where once a child's uncertainty beamed out, now a young man's questions darken his visage. It says very clearly to her, 'Is this enough for her? Will she leave it alone?' She drops her eyes. 'Yes,' she thinks, 'it is enough.'

The evening grows longer teeth. There is a noise from the wagon; Lupul rises and goes to the waking man. Taking his arm he leads him to the edge of the fire, the old blanket around his shoulders; he lowers him to the ground and with a few murmurs he is again asleep. Ana checks the wrappings on the wounds which are healing but still dark and crusted with blood; they will have to be changed tomorrow morning before they continue or the wounds will fester and he will die. She touches his sleeping face, so like the face of her dreams and memories before this all began. A single tear climbs down the wrinkled slope that is now Ana's cheek.

Two more days bring them to the pass overlooking their home. It is evening. "We need to avoid the main paths. We need to get him to the caves without anyone seeing us. Do you know the way?" She speaks over her shoulder to Lupul, who this day has been walking behind.

"Yes." She waits as he looks around then indicates her right, and passing her takes the lead.

She turns Stony off the beaten trail and ascends the much narrower and less used animal path leading around the valley. She knows they will soon have to leave the cart and drape the unconscious Cain over the small pony to continue, but they must first hide the cart from prying eyes, in the bush away from the road. They leave the cart in a pine thicket and Lupul takes care of the tracks, leaving none for their pursuers to follow. He again takes the lead after tying a cut branch to the saddle to drag behind the pony, further hindering tracking.

The going is harder that day and with great weariness they make camp that night beneath a great old cedar, breaking off the lower dead branches for the small, smokeless fire. With the low bent branches blocking a good share of the light from the fire, they cook a stew of salted meat and some wild roots Lupul brings back.

After eating, Cain joins them at the fire. His color and strength are greatly depleted from the rough travel stretched over the pony's back like a bag of oats. Ana feeds the soup to him slowly, sip by sip, and then attending his wounds, notices the red and swollen look of the worst.

She sits late into the night, sipping mint tea, thinking of the next part of their plan.

By noon the next day they find themselves at the base of a defile leading to the caves. The caves are part of a vast cavern complex that her village has used many times to hide in as they are very well hidden. Soon they are uncertain if the pony is more of a burden and wonder if carrying Cain would not be easier than continuing as they are, but one look at Cain's worsening condition convinces Ana that the speed of the little pony over the obstacles more than makes up for the pushing and coaxing needed to get him to keep going.

By the last dying rays of light they arrive at the entrance to the warrens. They descend into a deeper darkness to find a smooth flat floor just around the first turn in the dark cave. Lupul steps to the wall; reaching into a crevice he removes a bundle. He shakes it onto the floor and in a few moments has a blazing torch in his hand. Ana looks around the space then and is amazed at the store of provisions stacked neatly on shelves carved into the natural rock walls. Lupul finds a hole chiseled into the wall to hang the torch.

In one corner of the great chamber is a natural fireplace.

She and Lupul take Cain from the pony and lower him onto one of the rock shelves, laying him on the old blanket. He is delirious with a raging fever. For the first time Ana fears for his life; she has nothing to treat him. A quick once-over of the supplies in the cavern's extensive shelves and crevices reveal bandages but no salves or the all important willow bark to help him.

She takes Lupul's arm, pulling him to the entrance of the cavern. She cannot make herself meet his eyes; what she has to ask him she is afraid he will refuse to do. But she has to try. "Will you go home and bring mama's medicine bag? I need it if he is to live."

He looks at her. His eyes are dark, and his mind is sharp to her distress. He takes her chin in his hand. Lifting it he makes her meet his eyes, "Yes, for you." And then he is gone, into the night; just one shadow among their kindred.

If Cain's need was not so great and time so limited she would let herself weep with the love she feels now, and the relief.

She returns to the main chamber. Cain is lying stretched out on the floor now, rolling back and forth and tearing at his head. His fingers find the greatest pain and after tearing loose the bandages, dig into the newly crusted scabs letting blood flow. He moans from the pressure in his head, the fire in his mind. She approaches and he strikes out at her with hands smeared in his own blood; he misses with the first strike but then deals a resounding slap to her face leaving a bloody streak. She pulls away. He rolls over again and then she is on him holding him on his belly, face in the dirt. Her weight is easily enough to subdue him in this weakened state. His struggling subsides and he seems to settle into a restless sleep. She drags him back to the bed and once there rests herself a moment on its edge beside him.

After catching her breath she goes to the supplies and takes out the great cooking pot; so much a staple for cooking and life of the village, she knew it would be there. She swings it onto its place near the open fireplace; she takes a few minutes to get a good fire going. When she stops in her preparations for a moment she again sees Cain on the ground struggling on his belly for the door, blood and dirt striping his face and hands. She rushes over and again gets him back onto the shelf. Again he drops into sleep.

She goes back to the alcove to finish her preparations. The fire is hot in the stuffy cave but the smoke finds its way up a crack in the ceiling and into the open night. As the kettle heats Ana puts the last of the water in it, filling it about halfway.

She goes back to Cain then; he has not moved this time but she is surprised to find his eyes open, staring at her. As she approaches she cowers. His face melts into abject terror and he begins to cry, the soft sobs of a child in pain. In a moment the sobs subside into deep breathing.

She turns back to the kettle and finds the water simmering. She picks up the discarded bandages and, taking some others from the stores, tosses them into the hot water. Stirring them together she makes sure the water has a chance to cook them well before, using a wooden spoon, she lifts them from the water and drapes them over a piece of rope she has set up just for this. They hang dripping and steaming. She then takes the kettle from its hook and with her hands wrapped with her apron carries it outside the cave to pour the dirty water down the slope. On her way back to the mouth of the cave she walks silently, listening; she knows there is water here but cannot remember where. She listens to the sounds of the night for any idea of where it might be. The silence descends around her like a blanket; she reaches out with her senses. Ah, there it is: a faint gurgling in the quiet night. She moves off the trail and there, a small spring bubbles up from the rocks and flows into a natural basin. She takes the big kettle and bracing herself, dips it down into the water, taking as much as she can lift and carry with her back to the cave.

She finds Cain again on the floor crawling toward the entrance when her eyes adjust to the firelight. She steps over his now still form and puts the water back on the hook, this time away from the fire's heat, then turns to care for Cain.

The night continues like this.

In the early hours just before dawn she drifts off for a moment. At this point Cain, in his delirium, again wakes but this time with a monstrous power. He sits up, crossing to where she leans on the wall exhausted, slumber winning out. He grabs her and throws her to the ground. She awakens stunned with the impact to find him standing over her holding a rock in his hand, ready to bring it crashing down on her head.

Dawn reaches the entrance of the cave and with it the shadow of Lupul; he appears with a savage growl. He rushes forward and crashes into Cain, the stone falling to the floor. He pins the delirious man to the floor holding his arms easily above his head with one hand and steadying his head with the other.

Ana returns to her senses as the shadow of a woman blocks the sun entering the cavern. She sits up from the floor. Turning her face she sees the woman approach, arms loaded with supplies and food.

Vaguely she recognizes the woman… her mother? It can't be; her mother died when she was birthing Lupul. As the woman comes closer Ana sees that it is not her mother but her younger sister. She rises to her feet, unsteady and exhausted, but very relieved to have help after the long night. She goes to her sister and hugs her, crying with relief.

Cain, unconscious again, is a limp weight in Lupul's arms as he puts him back on the stone shelf. He turns to Ana and is in time to catch her as she moves to his arms and hugs her back furiously. This has been a long night for both of them.

That day Ana rests as her sister takes over caring for them all. She regains her strength from the stew the young woman makes and the short hours of deep sleep between Cain's fits of lucid screaming and threats. Every hour he grows weaker; the medicines and care slow his decline but do not abate it. The evening brings them all together sipping hot tea. Ana, looking into the eyes of each of her siblings, finds there the same opinion. If something doesn't change soon, Cain will not survive the night.

Her chest heaves with the thought of losing him. She cannot stand to be inside any more so she stands and walks to the cave's entrance. Finding the path in the early dusk she ascends. The path takes her to the top of the mountain. The walk takes a few minutes as it winds up, the scrub brush disappearing into barren rock. The wind picks up.

On the peak she drops to her knees with her hands before in supplication. She stays that way praying that she will have strength for what is to come, praying for the will to keep fighting. From out of the darkness, a man approaches up the trail, his cane clicking on the rocks as he moves swiftly, until he is before her; just two breaths. Used to his quickness and sudden appearance she only looks at him, sorrow written in the lines of her face.

He sinks to his knees in front of her taking her hands in his own. "My child," he starts, "yours is a very difficult path with nothing but nightmare and horror before you. Would that I could take this from you. Would that I could take you away from this or do this deed for you, but it is not for me... this doom. It is the price that must be paid to rid the world of a great evil." With this he takes her worn tired hands and kisses them. Then taking her in his arms he kisses her head and holds her, warming her from the wind with his cloak. The smell of the forest surrounds him; she takes it in and is strengthened by it.

He pulls back from her. Holding her hands he draws her up with him. They stand like this a moment; she draws strength from him.

Out of the night comes a sound, distant thunder, followed by the ominous growl of a large predator. Ana clutches at the old man but finds herself holding empty air. Then she hears, "This is how it begins; be brave."

Across the peak from her she sees an unbelievably large beast moving fast in a galloping gait across the rock, leaping chasms and bounding from boulder to boulder. Ana is frozen with fright; she knows to run is only to postpone her death.

From the trail comes another sound like the first but more human; it ends in a long howl like a great wolf. Lupul is at her side, bow drawn and ready. His eyes glow with coming battle, his body is stiff and braced.

The bear stops a short five meters from them; Ana, hands balled at her side holding her ground, Lupul between her and the bear, ready to release the first arrow. The bear's eyes look out of a face grizzled with half a century's battles, more than one with men like Lupul. But he holds back. There is something about this man; he smells of wolf, he is not running. All the men before had run from his great size and mighty teeth and claws. He sniffs the air again. Yes, there is more here than just the man he faces.

With a lunge the great bear attacks. "Ana! Go back to the cave!" Lupul lets fly the first arrow; it strikes above the beast's shoulder biting into the fur and gristle without noticeable effect. He has another arrow in the air almost before the first strikes; this one sinks deep into the space by the bear's neck.

The first lunge took the beast half the distance separating them, but the second arrow hurts and he turns a little and slows.

Ana takes off down the trail as fast as her feet can move, into the night; she feels deep pain for her brother but also great pride in his strength standing before the bear, silhouetted by the flashing lightning and the bear's roars accented by the thunder. Above all she has never felt more fear for anyone than now. But her purpose is clear and the feeling that time is running out is strong in her mind.\

In moments she arrives at the cave's mouth; she stops and listens. She hears Cain talking to her sister in low tones; her sister answers. She enters and finds Cain lying on the bed, his eyes open and clear, but she is also aware of another power in the cave, a malignant presence. Immediately she understands Cain's recovery.

She enters the great chamber and approaches Cain on the shelf. She looks down on him, and he sits up and looks at her, then stands on shaky legs. They embrace for a moment. She can feel him, the old Cain, back in her arms. She utters a soft cry of joy and holds him close, her sister looking on with a tear in her eye. She pulls back a little to see his eyes in the cave's flickering light.

She is stunned for a moment but before she can respond he pushes her to the ground! She falls and gasps in shock. Her sister attacks him from behind holding him off just long enough for Ana to crawl to her feet and escape the cave into the night.

Out in the dark she slips around to the little cove in the rock where the spring pushes water gurgling into the basin. She drops to her knees in the warm soft earth beside the water and addresses herself to the hidden one, knowing she can hear her. "Release him! He is not for you; he is my love and I will do what I have to do to protect him from you!"

There is a flicker from the wall beside Ana and then a shadow takes shape. Ana feels the kick coming before it lands; the wind is taken from her chest in a single blast as the witch kicks her. She rolls and comes up against the rock wall. The witch is there in her face, whole and solid now. "No, he is mine; you may have thwarted me in the castle with your meddling but not here. Here he is mine and he will stay mine."

Ana meets her eyes, brown to black, and a long moment passes when neither flinches nor turns. Then the witch smiles; a cruel smile. "Alright, I accept your offer." She raises her arm and strikes Ana on the cheek; her nail draws blood. Ana turns away, holding her hand on her bleeding cheek. The witch turns to the seeping spring. Flicking her hand over the water she utters a few words in a guttural language Ana has never heard before. There is a swirling of the water and then all is still. The witch begins to cackle. There is a flash of lightning and Cain appears. The witch is gone.

Cain comes to her as she gets to her feet. She feels very strange, everything is slowing. The flashing of the lightning is making everything surreal. There is pain, the slow grinding pain of her body turning to stone. Then he is there. Cain is back; his arms are gentle but passionate, his eyes cry and the tears mix with the pouring rain. He holds her as she begins to change. She kisses him one last time as the transformation takes her and she is taken away. She reaches for him, tries to hold him still as her arms lose their ability to move.

Cain:

It all comes back to him as the witch releases her control of him, with one thing to do. He rushes from the cave out into the dark and rain. Too late to stop it, too late to save his love; he sees the price she has paid for him. His chest heaves with the restoration of their love all at once, bringing with it the burden of all the pain and remorse for all his actions. It staggers him but still he gets to her before she is gone. The light is still in her eyes when he reaches her but all is stone, hard and cold to his touch. The rain mixes with her tears as she reaches for him across the water. He touches her only to see the final light leave her as the stone traps her and she is gone.

Chapter Eight

Cain:

Every year he goes to her on this day, the anniversary of her transformation. He stays in the village she grew up in. He uses his skills as a woodsman, and later as a carver, to earn a living and take care of his wife. He married her sister and they have a daughter; he names her Ana after her aunt, his first love.

That night still haunts him; he can hear her voice speaking to him whenever he is here with her. At first it was only a whisper on the wind, a haunting reminder of her, then each time he came back her voice would sing to him or try to calm his ragged lament and his self abasement over that night so many years ago now. She it was who convinced him to move on and gave him her blessing to marry her sister, wanting neither to live on in the torturous knowledge of her imprisonment in stone; that she would not be happy until they were also. After many years she stopped talking to them because the pain was too great, the loss too mortal for any of them.

He continued to visit her alone every year until this year, the seventeenth year after her imprisonment; his daughter's fifteenth birthday.

Taking her hand he leads Ana up the narrow, steep path to the little corner where her tears eternally fill the little cistern of rock. Years ago he had planted beautiful creeping roses but now they threaten to take over the entire side of the mountain with their lovely pink and white blossoms. He takes her to this garden where he put a pleasant little oak bench in the shade, a place to sit and rest when he visits with her; another of her suggestions, when she would talk to him.

This year he is here to tell his daughter the story of that fateful night, hopeful that Ana herself will participate and introduce herself to the young woman who so resembles her namesake. He prays she will: it has been so many years since he last heard her voice; he misses her.

He begins the story with Ana turning to stone in his arms and tells her of his love, and that he screamed challenges to the witch, cried out his hate and anger until his voice failed him. Then dropping to his knees before her he swore his eternal devotion to her memory, thinking her dead.

Then there was a light, almost timid, touch to his shoulder. Thinking it the witch he spun, ready to strike. A moment it took for him to realize it was her sister, young Ana's mother. Relief flooded him and he released his clenched fists. Then he saw the look on her face: grief and shock mingled with urgency. She tried to speak but the words would not come. Taking her by the elbows he tried to calm her, and then asked what was wrong. She turned, breaking away, and led him up the mountain in a rush.

At the top of the peak appeared to them such a tableau, even all these years later it is one he can only utter as a sketchy description and in simple terms, its horror something his mind can only relate in pieces. Ana's mother still cannot speak of it and would not let him tell the story at all until this year.

Lupul had fought the great bear to save his sister. When the bear got too close for arrows he had held the great beast off with his knife in one hand and a rock in the other; so they had found him, still armed. The battle had been bloody and long there was no doubt. That either could be said to win or lose God would have to decide, for neither gave in. Lupul had died in the great bear's embrace. Later the village men had to cut them apart.

After the story, he sat with her for a few minutes hoping that the older Ana would take the time to talk to the young woman, say something, and feed his starving hope a crumb. But starvation would be its demise.

After a few minutes the young woman stands from her father, pats him on the head and leaves him alone to wander the glade and look at the roses as they grow all along the track. She heads up the trail toward the cave.

She is gone a few moments when he stands and walks to stand across from the fair features of the smooth stone. Close to her, so his whispers will not be overheard by his daughter, he says, "My love, all these years I come to you and beg a word or a sound from you so I can know you are still alive and that there is still hope to free you. Maybe in her death the witch's spell can be broken. Something, my love, to keep me believing." Silence answers his plea. He turns to take his seat again, ever patient.

Then he hears a scream from up the path. His pulse pounding in his ears, he races up the trail, the sure knowledge of his daughter's voice as the originator powering his old limbs. At the mouth of the cave he is captured in a grip of air so strong he can hardly breathe. His daughter faces an old woman in flowing black robes, long and tattered. The woman, seeming to float off the ground, holds a pearl of pulsing light before Ana's eyes in one hand and a plump ripe cherry before her gaping mouth in the other.

So powerful is his dismay and horror, his will momentarily overcomes the magic holding him and he gasps out, "No, not again!" Then he is held again in that tightening grasp. His mind racing, he bashes against the bonds while each second the damned cherry gets closer and closer to his baby girl's blanched lips. From where he finds the strength he does not know, but with all his strength he reaches out to the only other help on the mountain. He again breaks the bonds just long enough to utter one word, "Ana!"

Three things happen all at once; later they would come back to him in dreams. But then they happened too fast for his perception. There is a flash of light from the mountain itself, bright enough to stun and leave a ghost image on the eye long after the event; Ana appeared from her glade, in such beauty and light, to make the bright day as a flash of lightning is to a storm darkened night. She glides from her fountain and ascends the mountain lighting up the world around her, passing him with a light gossamer touch and a fleeting smile.

Her countenance changes to one of anger as she confronts the witch. She places herself between the witch and her quarry, very close yet not touching. The witch steps back; the globe of green light disappears along with the cherry. She begins to chant and mumble in the deep and malignant language, moving her hands, shaping shadows and mist.

Ana confronts the glare and spell-casting of the witch with disdain. She points her finger at little Ana and with a motion sends her flying back to Cain, releasing him at the same time so he is able to catch her and fall with her to the dirt path.

Ana turns to her nemesis then and the two face off. On even footing with an adversary for the first time ever the witch shifts her stance and would run away, but Ana is ready for this; she reaches her hand out. As wind captures and manipulates fog so she contains the witch in the flow of her own power. She takes the creature held in this bubble back to the small cistern, the place of her imprisonment all these long years.

As the bubble holding the witch descends to hover over the little pool, Ana speaks to her. "All these years you left me captured in your spell crying tears to feed this cistern, and each year the pool has grown deeper. Alas, this year my tears overflow and I have enough to drown you." With this she pushes the struggling creature down into the water. There follows a stream of begging, piteous cries and weeping, then the hissing of steam as each tear takes a piece of the witch and she dissolves in the salty water of her own making. The last to be seen of her is the swirl of her cloak as it too melts in the cistern of shed tears.

Ana stands before her stone self watching the water drip from the statue's eyes, now an empty husk, after having finally escaped. She turns and winks at Ana, blows Cain a kiss, then disappears in a flash.

Jonela Tudor:

Resides in Bucharest, Romania and is studying to become a veterinarian. She has interests in mythology and fantasies. She is also the Muse, and the conception of this story was born in her.

Kim Chamberlin:

Resides in Virginia, USA and is a network engineer for a hospital system. He did the work. ☺